WAKING OF THE WITCH

WITCHES OF KEATING HOLLOW, BOOK 11

DEANNA CHASE

ABOUT THIS BOOK

Georgia Exler has always been the odd witch out. In a family
of accomplished witches, she's the only one who never
uncovered her own magical abilities... until she moved to
Keating Hollow. Heartbroken after her husband of two years is
killed in a tragic accident, the writer moves to the enchanted
town to start over. All she wants to do is write her next book
and make a few new friends. But when the events in her life
start to mimic the newest paranormal romance she's writing,
she starts to wonder if maybe she's found her magic after all.
Only how is she going to give her characters their happily-
ever-after, when she's terrified to finish because everything she
writes seems to come true?

Logan Malone has loved and lost not once, but twice. He's a
man who's resigned to a quiet single life among the redwoods
and his manuscripts of hope and new beginnings. What he
writes and what he's wants are two different things. Or so he
thinks. When another writer befriends him, suddenly magic is

in the air, and the walls he's built start to crumble. Is the third time a charm or will he leave Keating Hollow before he has a chance to find out?

CHAPTER 1

*G*eorgia Exler took a long sip of her pear martini and nearly spit it out when she heard her name being called from the newly built stage at the Keating Hollow Brewery.

"Come on, Georgia!" Hanna Pelsh smirked from her place under the spotlight. "It's time to pay up on that little bet we made last month. Now get your sassy butt up here and show us exactly what you've got."

No! Georgia mouthed, shaking her head at her now ex-friend. In a drunken moment of weakness, she'd made a bet with Hanna over who might turn up pregnant next in Keating Hollow. Something must have been in the magical waters of the town, because half the population seemed to be baby crazy. Hanna bet that Faith Townsend was next in line, while Georgia had speculated that Shannon and Brian looked like they were never going to leave the honeymoon phase, and that if they didn't take a breather, Shannon would be next. Sure enough, Faith had just announced she was three months along and was expecting her first child early the next year.

Which meant Georgia lost the bet. And the kicker? The payment required the loser to step out of her comfort zone by doing something she'd never done before, and the winner got to choose what that activity would be.

Georgia deeply regretted ever telling her friend that she was a karaoke virgin who had no desire to ever stand on a stage and make a fool of herself.

That was the last time she'd ever confide anything to Hanna Pelsh.

"Aww, looks like Georgia is a little shy." Hanna flashed the rest of the patrons an engaging smile. "I think she needs a little encouragement, don't you? Georgia! Georgia! Georgia!" she chanted.

The crowd joined in, bringing the noise level in the bar up to a nearly unbearable level.

Georgia grimaced but forced herself to her feet, knowing that she wasn't going to be getting out of this one without looking like a complete coward. That was the last thing she was going to do, especially considering the fact that her fellow writer, Logan Malone, was sitting in the corner and watching her with interest. She was going to murder Hanna for setting her up to look like a fool in front of that gorgeous man.

Gritting her teeth, Georgia made her way to the small stage. Once she was standing next to Hanna, she whispered, "I hope you have your life insurance in order."

Hanna just laughed, her dark eyes full of mischief. "I'm not worried." She winked at Georgia before nodding to Candy, her younger cousin who was manning the karaoke machine. "Hit it."

The poppy beat of Madonna's "Like a Virgin" filled the brewery, making Georgia groan. She loved vintage Madonna as much as the next girl, but it was not a tune she could pull off without sounding like a frog who needed throat lozenges. She put her hand up, indicating she needed a moment, and then walked over to Candy to make a request. Candy nodded and got busy changing the song.

When the dreamy melody of "Landslide" by Fleetwood Mac started to play, Georgia felt a sort of spell come over her. She got lost in the music, forgetting about the crowd that had chanted so enthusiastically for her only moments ago. The bar and all its patrons disappeared as she slipped back into the time after she'd gotten the call that her husband had died in a skiing accident. In the days that followed, all she'd been able to do was listen to his favorite band and pray that Nick would show up and explain it had all been a horrible mistake.

Only that hadn't ever happened. Instead, she'd memorized every word of every song on *The Dance* album in an effort to feel closer to the husband she'd loved with everything she'd had.

The music flowed through her, and Georgia allowed herself to sink into the notes, singing with all her heart. She felt the sting of tears come but paid it no attention. She was singing the song for Nick and somehow feeling close to him again, as if he'd never left her. The warmth of his remembered embrace was all too real. She basked in it, letting her heart feel whole again.

But then the music suddenly stopped mid-note, and Candy let out a muttered curse about the defective karaoke machine. "Hold on, Georgia. It'll take me just a second to reset the music."

The spell that had washed over Georgia completely vanished, leaving her trembling on the stage with fresh tears on her cheeks as she stared out at the now silent patrons of the bar. She opened her mouth to apologize for the interruption, but no words came out. Her limbs were frozen, and panic started to set in, the same panic that had overcome her when she'd first learned of Nick's sudden passing.

Georgia turned, ready to flee the stage, but before she could take even one step, she spotted Logan Malone bounding up onto the stage. He grabbed a guitar off a stand and moved toward her, already strumming the notes to the song she'd been singing.

Logan gave her an encouraging smile and said, "I know I speak for everyone here when I ask you to please finish that wonderful rendition of "Landslide.""

"I don't—" she started, but as his fingers continued to strum over the strings of the guitar, the panic started to fade and her rapid pulse stabilized. Logan held her gaze and nodded his encouragement.

Georgia stared into his silver-gray eyes and let the music move through her. The pain of her loss was still there, but focusing on Logan dulled that ache in her heart and kept her present in the moment instead of thrusting her back into a time that had been filled with so much pain that she'd thought she'd never recover. Her voice was raspy as she leaned into the lyrics, and for the first time since she'd lost Nick, a spark of true happiness lit in her soul. It was the love of music, of sharing her gift that she'd loved and lost right along with the death of her husband.

By the time she belted out the last note, there were tears in her eyes again. Only this time they were happy tears, and for the first time in months, she felt truly alive.

"Oh my goodness!" Hanna exclaimed into her handheld microphone. "I think if this was a talent show, we'd all know who won this evening. Wouldn't we?" she asked the crowd.

The room erupted into cheers, and someone let out a piercing whistle of approval.

Georgia felt her face heat with embarrassment, and suddenly she needed to be anywhere except on that stage. She gave the crowd a nod and a quick wave before rushing off the stage and out a side door of the brewery. The cool fall air hit her bare arms, and she took a deep breath, filling her lungs as she leaned against the cool cement wall of the building.

Her emotions were all over the place.

What the hell happened in there? she thought. First, she'd been swept up in memories of her husband, and then she'd been trapped in the silvery gaze of another man she barely knew. It both scared her and pissed her off.

The door swung open and Logan strode out, his long legs carrying him about ten feet before he stopped and glanced around for her.

Georgia tried to fade right into the cement wall, but she hadn't suddenly developed the ability to vanish into thin air, so he spotted her almost instantly.

Logan let out a relieved sigh and quickly joined her near the building. He draped his arm around her and pulled her in so that she was leaning against his shoulder. "Are you all right?"

"I'm fine," she said and gently pulled away from him. Only it wasn't because she didn't want to be close to him. On the contrary. His woodsy scent pulled her in and made her want to bury her head in his chest while he soothed circles into her lower back. The image was so vibrant that she could almost feel his hand on her even though she'd put more than an arm's length of distance between them.

"Are you sure?" he asked, his forehead wrinkling in concern. His voice was full of sympathy and tenderness when he continued. "That song and the emotion that was pouring out of you... It'd be enough to bring even me to my knees."

Georgia swallowed, trying to clear the lump in her throat. "I'm okay." But the words sounded hollow even to her own ears. She shrugged helplessly. "Maybe I'm still a little shaky, but I'll be fine. It's nothing I haven't been through before."

He nodded, sympathy swimming in that silver gaze of his. "It's strange how music just pulls emotion right out of us like that, isn't it?"

She let out a quiet chuckle. "I should have known better. I can't even listen to that song without tearing up."

"That's what made your performance so powerful. Thank you for putting your heart out there like that." He gave her a small smile that didn't quite reach his eyes. "Not many people do these days."

Georgia looked at the man in a new light, seeing for the first time the pain behind his kindness. She'd never call herself an empath, but in that moment, she felt a thread of his sadness buried deep inside of him, and she felt a connection to him that she hadn't ever felt to another person. Not even Nick. It made her want to wrap her arms around him and pull him in close, but she hesitated. She barely knew this man. That would definitely be weird, right? Instead, she reached out and squeezed his hand. "Thank you for saving me up there when the machine died. If you hadn't saved the day, I probably would've started making really bad dad jokes."

His silver eyes glinted. "Oh, yeah? Like what?"

Chuckling, she shook her head. "Oh no. We don't know each other nearly well enough for me to embarrass myself like that." She grinned, leaned in, and kissed him on the cheek. Sparks lit in her belly as her lips brushed across his stubbled cheek, and Georgia sucked in a breath of desire as Logan's hand landed on the small of her back. They stood there for a few seconds, watching each other. Her gaze landed on his full lips, and she couldn't help it when her tongue darted out to wet her own.

Logan cleared his throat, but his voice still came out slightly husky as he said, "That's too bad. I always love a really good dad joke." He stepped back, and suddenly she was cold, though she didn't think it was from the chill in the air. His lips turned down into a slight frown before he said, "It was good seeing you again. Goodnight, Georgia."

Then he turned and walked off into the parking lot.

Georgia stared after him, wondering what the hell had just happened.

CHAPTER 2

"Well, speak of the devil," Chad Garber said when Logan walked into Magical Notes, the town's only music store. He glanced at Levi, the young man behind the counter, and added, "I've never seen smoother moves than I did last night at the brewery when he got up onstage and started playing so Georgia could finish her song. The only question is why he didn't cash in on all that rock-star worship. Imagine if he'd let on that he was the lead guitarist for Jump Back. There'd have been panties dropping across three counties."

"Yeah, even Silas was swooning after I showed him the video," Levi replied, running a hand through his dark curly hair. His lips curved up into a smirk. "Good thing he's out of the country right now. I don't need the competition."

Logan rolled his eyes at the pair. He should've known they wouldn't let the previous evening's events go by without comment. Not after he'd confessed that before he became a writer he'd been in a band that had found success after recording a theme song for *Little Liam*, a kid's show that had run for over ten years on cable that had produced phrases such as *Bite my sass* and *Bring on the boogie*. "Funny. Keep it up and I'll take my business elsewhere."

Chad snorted. "Like you're going to drive all the way to Eureka for drum lessons from Hogan, the man who smokes so much weed he can't even remember what decade it is."

Chuckling, Logan shook his head. "Definitely not interested in trying lessons with Hogan again. But there's always online instruction."

All three of them knew Logan wouldn't make good on his threat. The truth was, Logan was already competent at drumming. He just liked brushing up on his skills and socializing with other musicians without having the pressure of being in a band. He'd done that before and wasn't interested in it again.

"Seriously, man," Chad said, a note of awe in his tone. "That was some damn fine playing last night. You've been holding out on us."

Logan shrugged. It had been years since he'd played in front of an audience. And it likely would have been years more if he hadn't suddenly found himself moved to help out his fellow writer. The moment he'd met Georgia Exler, he'd known she'd break through all his barriers. It was why he'd stayed away from the Incantation Café since that first day they'd met. She'd just been too... enticing. Logan had come to Keating Hollow to finish his latest book, not to get involved with another woman. He'd been there and done that. Twice. He was done. All he needed was his writing and music.

But his encounter with the gorgeous writer the night before had nearly broken his resolve. He'd been seconds from asking her out. Hell, he'd nearly pushed her up against the side of the brewery and kissed the life out of her. He couldn't remember when he'd wanted someone that badly. So instead, he'd done the only thing he could do. He'd gone home and stared at a blank page of his newest work in progress and convinced himself that sharing the quaint magical town with Georgia Exler would not drive him mad.

Too bad he'd gone to sleep thinking of her and had woken up after dreaming she'd been in his bed all night. That was why he'd come to Magical Notes. He needed to get his mind off her, and since writing hadn't worked, he figured learning a new song on the drums was the next best thing.

"I told you I was in a band," Logan said in response to Chad's comment about his guitar playing.

"Yeah, but your band didn't put out anything like what you did last night," Levi insisted. "That was some Lindsey Buckingham level of playing. Not the same three chords for a kid's song. Truly impressive."

Chad nodded. "Levi's right. Really fantastic man. If you ever want to jam, or teach, or hell, start a band, let me know. I'm all-in."

Logan laughed nervously. "I think you two might be laying it on thick, but thanks for the ego boost."

"No way, man," Levi said. "I'm with Chad. You two should start a band. I'd come listen for sure."

"Only if you joined us," Chad said to him. "You're getting really good on those drums."

Levi scoffed. "I can pound on a couple songs, but my skill isn't anywhere near the level of you or Logan. You'd be better off holding auditions for someone who has a lot more experience."

Chad shook his head. "Hell no." He turned to Logan. "I've never seen someone pick up the drums that fast. I think it has to do with his spirit magic. His timing is impeccable. Truly something special." Chad moved to sit behind a piano and started absently playing. He nodded to the other two. "Let's see how we sound."

Levi immediately moved behind a drum set and started tapping out a beat.

Logan stared at them and then smiled to himself when they started playing "Sweet Child O' Mine" by Guns N' Roses. How could he pass that up? The guitar riff was one of his favorites.

He walked over and picked up a white electric guitar, plugged it in, and picked at the strings until the cords overtook him like they always did. Music filled the shop, and Logan was completely lost to it, pouring everything he had into the song. His mind stilled and all his worries over this latest writer's block vanished. His soul filled with that magic that permeated him when he was creating something he loved. It was almost as if he was transported to another world, one where he was free from all the pain of his past and the future was full of promise.

He was just *alive*.

The three of them played their hearts out, and when the last note died away, silence filled the space until one person started a slow clap of appreciation.

Having just come out of his music haze, Logan turned, and his eyes widened when he spotted Georgia Exler standing in the shop with a look of wonder on her heart-shaped face. "Wow, and here I thought you were a writer. Sounds like you should be out on tour with Axl Rose."

Logan carefully placed the guitar back in its stand and shoved his hands into his back pockets. "We were just blowing off steam."

"Sounded like a recording session." She nodded to Chad and Levi. "Very well done. You should go out on the road."

Levi grinned. "That would be something, wouldn't it? Too

bad Chad has sworn off touring. Not to mention I have that internship at the clinic. But Logan here? He definitely deserves a spot in another band. One that isn't afraid to utilize his talent."

"Levi," Logan said in a warning tone.

"You were in a band?" Georgia asked, her expression full of interest. "I thought you used to run a nursery before you became a novelist?"

Dammit. Logan didn't like talking about his past. And he certainly didn't want to explain to anyone, let alone Georgia Exler, why he'd left the music industry. "Yes. Both are true. But that was a long time ago. It turns out my passion is with the written word instead of plants or chords on a guitar."

"That's unfortunate for me." She gave him a flirty smile. "I always wanted to date a musician. I guess I'll just have to keep looking. Too bad these two are already taken." She gestured to Chad and Levi. "Pretty sure Hope and Silas wouldn't care for a groupie fawning over their men."

Chad chuckled while Levi dropped one of his drumsticks and then flushed pink.

Levi's phone buzzed with a message. He pulled the phone out of his pocket and excused himself as he dialed. "Hey, Silas, great timing," he said as he disappeared into the back room.

"Thanks, man," Chad said, clapping Logan on the back. "I haven't had that much fun playing in ages. Anytime you want to get together just to play, let me know."

Logan nodded but knew he wasn't likely to take Chad up on the offer. Already he was feeling the crash from the high of playing his heart out. The old familiar pain started to creep back into his soul as he thought of the last night he'd been with his band back in LA. Not the kid's music band but the one that had been his ticket to a life onstage, playing the music he loved most. It was the night when he'd lost everything important to him and had thrust his life onto a completely different path than the one he'd always dreamed about.

He sighed, knowing he was in for a rough night of regret unless he figured out a way to keep his mind off the memories that so often haunted him after playing the guitar. What had he been thinking? Wasn't it bad enough that he'd played the night before? But somehow that had felt different, and the letdown that he'd been expecting hadn't come.

"Logan?" Georgia asked, her voice full of concern. "Are you all right?"

"What?" he asked, startled out of his thoughts.

"You look like you've been visited by a ghost," she said.

If only, he thought. He'd give anything to see her again, even in her spirit form. "Sorry," he said hastily. "Just thinking I should probably get back to work. You know how it is with editors breathing down your neck."

She gave him a sympathetic smile. "Deadline hell. I know it well." She patted his arm. "Good luck."

He nodded and turned to Chad. "Can we reschedule the drumming lessons? I really do need to get back to work."

"Of course," Chad said. "Just let me know when."

Logan said something about calling next week and then strode out of the shop. He headed straight back to his rental, but instead of opening his laptop to work on the book that really was overdue, he changed clothes, stuffed his feet into his running shoes, and bolted out the door, determined to pound out the miles until the unwanted memories were once again locked away in the recesses of his mind.

CHAPTER 3

"*W*here is she?" Georgia asked as she swept into Amelia's house on the hillside. "I can't wait to snuggle that little girl of yours."

Amelia chuckled, making her unruly blond curls bounce around her face. "You'll have to fight it out with Faith. She got here before you."

Georgia sighed. "That's not fair at all. I can't fight a pregnant woman. Now what am I supposed to do?"

"Wait your turn?" Faith Townsend said, walking into the living room with Kiara, Amelia's little girl, bundled in her arms. Faith was absolutely glowing from head to toe, and the small smile on her face warmed Georgia's heart. Pregnancy really agreed with her.

While Georgia had no desire to be a mother herself, she loved being the fun aunt. And that's exactly what she planned to be to Amelia's little girl. Not that the child didn't already have over a dozen women lined up to spoil her rotten. Keating Hollow was just that sort of town.

"Fine. I'll wait you out. Surely, you'll need a nap soon, right?" Georgia teased.

Faith chuckled as she carefully took a seat on the couch, doing her best not to jostle the baby. "You're not wrong about that. I swear, I'm like a toddler these days. One minute I'm fine, and the next I'm having a meltdown that ends with a three-hour nap."

"Three hours? Are you sure there's only one in there?" Amelia asked. "I met a woman in the hospital who'd just had twins. She said she slept through most of her first and second trimester."

"Um…" Faith bit her bottom lip and gave them a nervous smile.

"Oh. Em. Gee," Amelia said in a hushed tone. "You *are* having twins, aren't you?"

Faith shook her head. "Triplets. The fertility doctor said it was a possibility, but I never thought it would actually happen, especially just a month after starting fertility meds. We'd been trying for a couple of years. The healer said the first thing to try was fertility meds to jumpstart my system since Hunter's swimmers are fine." She rolled her eyes. "He's very proud, let me tell you."

"Whoa," Georgia said. "Three babies. That's a lot all at once."

"It is, but I'll be honest and say that I'm thrilled, if not a little terrified," Faith admitted. "I've always wanted a big family."

"Well, you're on your way," Amelia said, her eyes wide as she stared at her friend. "I don't want to scare you, but just this one has been kicking my ass. The not sleeping at night thing is… Well, Grayson and I are both exhausted almost all the time."

Georgia took a closer look at her friend, noting the fatigue lining her eyes. But still, there was no missing the soft smile when Amelia glanced at her daughter. "Time moves so fast," Georgia said. "Before you know it, she'll be a teenager and the lack of sleep will be a distant memory. Then you'll be wishing she'd curl up with you for an afternoon nap."

Amelia snorted out a laugh. "I'm sure that's true, but right now, I'd kill for an uninterrupted thirty-minute nap."

"So go," Faith said, nodding toward the hallway. "We've got Kiara covered. It's not like you're getting her back while us greedy aunties are here anyway."

"She's not wrong," Georgia said, taking a seat next to Faith. "I haven't even gotten my hot little hands on her yet. You might as well take that nap while you still can."

Amelia hesitated, clearly torn on what to do. She glanced toward her bedroom and then back at her daughter.

"Go," Georgia urged. "At least go lay down and rest even if you don't sleep."

"I can't just go nap. That would be rude," she said.

"No, it isn't," Faith and Georgia said at the same time, making both of them chuckle. "We're here for you, not to be entertained by you," Faith added.

"She's right, you know," Georgia said as she eyed Amelia with a glint of amusement. "And next year when she has three of these, she'll be expecting you to return the favor."

"Oh boy. Then I better take what I can get while I can." She walked over to Faith, pressed a soft kiss to her daughter's head, and then waved as she shuffled down the hall. "Wake me up if you need anything at all."

"No way," Georgia called. "We've got this handled." Once Amelia closed the door to her bedroom, Georgia turned to Faith. "Have you ever done this before?"

"Done what? Watch a baby?"

"Yeah. Feed one, change a diaper, you know, the basics?" Georgia asked.

"Of course, I have. You are familiar with my family, right? Between Noel and Abby, I've been an aunt for some years now. Not to mention Yvette and Jake have Skye. I'm the go-to aunt at family gatherings."

Georgia had no doubt that was the case. Faith had wanted kids for a long time. Playing the doting aunt was right up her alley. "Okay, then let me hold the sleeping baby. When she wakes up, we can switch again."

Faith snickered. "Nice try, Georgia. I'm not giving up this snuggly bundle no matter what you say. But when she needs that diaper change, I'll gladly help you do it."

"You're so kind," Georgia said sarcastically and fervently hoped that the baby slept just as long as her mother.

"I aim to please." She grinned at Georgia. "Now, can we talk about those chapters you sent me for your newest book?"

Georgia's gut clenched. It wasn't often she let others read her work before she was ready to publish, but this one had her second guessing herself and she'd wanted a fresh pair of eyes just for a little perspective. Now that Faith had feedback, Georgia was certain she didn't want to hear it. Still, she knew after her years as an author that there was nothing better than raw, honest opinions... even if she ultimately decided to disregard whatever her friend had to say. "Hit me. What did you hate about it?"

"Hate?" Faith scoffed. "Please. I devoured those chapters. And when Ace found Heather in the woods after she twisted her ankle?" She sighed dreamily. "The way he carried her off to his cabin in the woods and barely kept himself contained while he helped her out of her muddy jeans and wrapped her ankle, I swear…" She fanned herself. "I had to wake Hunter up so the man could take care of some serious needs. I've never been so turned on by just the promise of a touch before. Hot, Georgia. Seriously hot. Hunter's really looking forward to when you send the payoff scene when they finally get together. No doubt my libido is going to be off the charts."

Oh, hell. This was a lot more than I bargained for, Georgia thought. Her face flushed hot, and she had to force herself not to avert her gaze. Georgia was a damned romance author. She ought to be able to have a conversation about the sex she wrote about, right? Wrong. She'd hadn't expected to learn that her friend's sex life was fueled by words she'd written. Georgia pasted on a smile. "That's good then, right?"

"Very good," Faith laughed. "I bet I wouldn't have needed fertility drugs if I'd been reading more of your books over the past two years."

Georgia groaned. "Stop. You're making me uncomfortable now."

Snickering, Faith patted her arm. "I can't help that you're *that* good of a writer."

"Thanks. It's just always weird for me to talk about the sexy parts of my books. I know that sounds prudish, but I can't help it. Thanks for reading and giving me an honest opinion. Was there anything that felt off or awkward?"

"Nope. But someday you're going to need to explain to me what it is about shifters that makes them so damned sexy."

"That's easy," Georgia said, happy to talk about anything other than her friend's sex life. "It's the growly, sexy, caveman thing, only in wolf form. Protective, alpha male, but soft and tender for only the heroine. It's catnip for us women. Taming the beast, that sort of thing."

"If I wasn't already with Hunter, I'd be out in those woods

everyday looking for my own growly man to rescue me," Faith said. "I mean, who wouldn't?"

"I could do without the sprained ankle," Georgia said. "Also, I don't love the idea of having to be rescued in real life. The book fantasy is always better."

"Eh, if there was a healer nearby, I wouldn't mind so much." Faith glanced down at Kiara as she stretched her small hands over her head and yawned. When the baby settled, she looked up again. "Levi's good at that sort of thing."

"I'll be sure to keep him on speed dial just in case I run into any trouble on my hike in the morning." Georgia gestured to the baby. "Hand her over. It's my turn for some snuggles."

Faith reluctantly agreed and carefully passed her over.

Georgia stared down at the baby, enjoying the sweet expression on her face as she continued to sleep. Her heart squeezed a little painfully as she wondered what her life would have been like if she'd had kids with Nick. It wasn't the path they'd chosen for themselves, and although she didn't regret their life in anyway, she couldn't deny that a part of her was melancholy for the family she'd always thought she could choose later if she wanted to.

"You and Kiara look awfully sweet," Amelia said from behind them. "You're good with her."

Georgia glanced back at her friend. "It's only because she's sleeping."

Chuckling, Amelia shook her head. "We both know she isn't. You've been making faces at her for the last few minutes and she's transfixed."

It was true, but Georgia would be hard pressed to admit it. She didn't like other people knowing she was a soft touch.

Amelia moved to sit on the arm of the couch. "I had a vision a few moments ago."

"You did?" Faith asked, her eyes wide. "What did you see?"

"Georgia in her house with a ring on her finger and stuffed animals strewn across the floor."

"What?" Georgia blinked at Amelia, her heart racing. "You did not. You're not even a seer, are you? I thought you were a fire witch."

She shrugged. "I started having visions when I was pregnant with Kiara. They stayed with me. I guess pregnancy can have an effect on magical abilities."

"Wow. Sounds like there are big changes coming your way, Georgia," Faith said, her eyes gleaming with excitement.

"No they aren't," Georgia said decisively. "I was married once. It's not happening again. The stuffed animals probably belong to someone else, like Kiara here, because there's no way children are in my near future."

"But they could be," Amelia said gently. "If you were open to it."

At just that moment, Kiara let out a cry of protest as she reached for her mother, clearly done with being doted on by her self-proclaimed aunties.

Georgia took it as a sign. Whatever Amelia had seen, she'd interpreted it wrong. Because there was no way Georgia was getting married or having kids. That ship had sailed.

CHAPTER 4

$\mathcal{T}$he sun heated Logan's face as he emerged from the redwoods into a clearing near the river. Thanks to the ten-mile run he'd pounded out the night before, his calves ached. But he still hadn't been able to handle staying cooped up in his house. Every time he tried to sit down and write, he heard Georgia asking him about his time in a band. Then the memories started to creep in again.

He just needed to clear his head and come up with an opening for his new book. The best way to do that was to get out from behind the computer screen and figure out what the hero's journey would be. His favorite trope was writing about the ordinary man who finds out he's the key to saving the world from the big evil. He'd written it before and was certain he'd write it again. He just needed to find a fresh angle. In his current state of mind, he was heavily leaning toward writing a dystopian. Maybe about found family living in the redwoods who were being threatened by a supernatural creature and the hero has a hidden power to stop the creature.

Logan mulled over the possibilities: haunted forest,

dragons as allies, and immortal death-bringers who prey on souls. The opening of the story was starting to form in his mind when he heard a sudden cry followed by the unmistakable sound of someone scrambling as the earth shifted under their feet.

He quickened his pace, moving faster into the thicket of trees. The trail wound upward and around a large boulder.

"Son of a bitch!" an all too familiar voice called out.

"Georgia?" he called back. "Is that you?"

"Logan?"

He hurried around the boulder and found Georgia sprawled on the ground, red dirt covering her black yoga pants and hiking shoes. "Are you all right?"

She stared up at him, a strange expression on her face.

"Georgia?" He kneeled down next to her and scanned her limbs for any sign of injury. "Are you hurt?"

"Oh, no. I don't think so." She pulled her legs in and planted her feet on the ground. "I just slipped. Can you help me up?"

He couldn't help noticing that her right hand and arm were scraped and blood was seeping from her palm. "Hold on." He reached into his back pocket and pulled out a bandana he kept there in case he needed something to keep the sweat out of his eyes, and he carefully began to wrap her hand.

She hissed when he tightened the fabric.

"Sorry." He grimaced, hating that he'd caused her more pain. "That will need to be cleaned, but hopefully that will stop the bleeding."

Georgia nodded. "I didn't even realize I was bleeding. Thanks."

"No thanks needed." He wrapped his hand around her left one and tugged, helping her to her feet.

She rose easily, but the moment she put weight on her right

foot, she let out another cry and nearly tumbled over. If he hadn't been there to catch her, she likely would've slid down the rest of the short hill. "Dammit! I sprained my ankle," she said, her eyes full of pain and frustration. "How am I going to get back to my house? I can't walk on it."

"I've got you. Don't worry." Logan slipped his arm around her waist and then the other one under her legs and pulled her up against his chest. "Wrap your hands around my neck. That will help."

She did as he asked, but still, she objected. "You can't carry me like this the entire way. I'm far too heavy for that."

"No, you aren't," he said even as his muscles protested. He had lifted her with relative ease, but carrying her all the way back to the trailhead might prove to be a bit of a challenge.

"Logan," she chastised. "We should call for help. Don't throw your back out trying to get me home."

"Grab my phone. It's in my back pocket." He concentrated on the trail as he moved downhill, careful not to lose his footing.

Georgia slid her hand down his back, causing a shiver to crawl up his spine. What was it about this woman that affected him so much? He'd never had such an instant physical connection with someone. Not even Cherry, the woman he considered the love of his life.

"No signal," she said and slipped the phone back into his pocket before wrapping her hands around his neck again.

"Then it looks like I'm getting more of a workout than I bargained for," he said, lengthening his stride as the trail flattened out.

"I'm so sorry, but thank you," Georgia said, sounding wary for the first time. "If you hadn't come along... I'd still be sitting in the dirt wondering what to do."

"Lucky timing," he said, already feeling a little winded.

"Do you hike out here often?" she asked, leaning her head against his shoulder.

"A few times a week. When I'm working on plot usually." He tightened his hold on her and tried not to think about the ache in his arms.

"Same," she said. "I just can't believe this happened and that you were the one to find me."

He wasn't sure how to answer her statement, so he didn't and instead just concentrated on getting her back to his car and to a healer as soon as possible.

By the time they emerged from the woods, the sun had moved behind dark gray clouds and large rain drops had just started to fall.

"Seriously?" Georgia said under her breath. "Rain?"

"It's okay," Logan said dismissively. "My SUV is right here. I'll get you to the local healer in no time."

"You don't have to do that," she said. "I can drive myself."

He scoffed. "It's your right ankle. I'll take you and get someone to come back with me for your car later."

"Logan, I—"

He cut her off. "Georgia. You're not driving. It isn't safe."

"All right," she said softly.

"Thank you," he breathed out, grateful that she was letting him take care of her. Because there was no way he was leaving her on her own. The thought of her driving with an injured foot terrified him.

"You're the one taking care of me," she said with a weak chuckle.

"Speaking of which, let's get you in this vehicle and to the healer. That ankle is the size of a softball." Logan tucked her into the back of his SUV, made sure her foot was elevated, and then drove her straight to the healer's office in Keating Hollow, only to find that Martin and Gerry Whipple were out of town for a few days. There was a note on the door indicating they should call the healer in Eureka.

But Logan took one look at Georgia's trembling form and swallowed the curse on his tongue. "Wait here. I'll be right back."

"As if I'm going to walk off somewhere?" he heard her say as he jogged down the street to Musical Notes in search of the only other person in town who he thought might be able to help.

The chimes sounded on the door as Logan walked into the music shop, and he let out a relieved breath when he spotted Levi Kelley behind the counter.

"Hey, man. Are you here to jam again?" Levi asked with an easy smile. "Chad's not here but—"

"No." Logan shook his head. "Georgia Exler hurt her ankle, and we need a healer. The Whipples are out of town."

Levi didn't hesitate. He nodded, grabbed his keys from a drawer, and quickly locked up before following Logan to his SUV.

Logan stood back and waited as the young man climbed into the back of the SUV to take a look at her ankle. Anxiety washed over him, and despite his fatigued body, he paced the sidewalk, trying to work off the nervous energy.

Eventually, his stomach grumbled, and he decided that Georgia must be starving too, so he walked a block down the street and ordered them Greek pizza and a salad from Mystyk Pizza. When he got back to his SUV, he found Georgia in the passenger seat and Levi standing in the open door saying something about Silas and how his latest movie was breaking box office records.

"He's getting all kinds of offers," Levi continued with a sad smile. "I'm pretty sure after all the promo he'll be doing, I won't get to see him unless I travel down to LA a few times. This long-distance bullshit sucks. Hard."

Georgia placed a hand over his, caressing his knuckles. "I'm sure he'd be here with you if he could."

"He would," Levi agreed. "I know that. But it doesn't change the fact that there's an ache in my chest now that he's gone all the time."

"Come here." Georgia opened her arms, inviting him in for a hug. The pair embraced, and Logan was certain he saw tears in both their eyes when they finally let go.

Logan's heart swelled with affection for the woman comforting Levi. He'd always been attracted to the ones who were genuinely kind. There was no question that Georgia cared deeply about the people around her. She was also smart, funny, a great writer, and an excellent friend. Not to mention gorgeous, though that was secondary to everything else. And Logan knew in that moment that he was falling for her.

"Oh, hell," he muttered.

Georgia released Levi and glanced back at him. "Problem?" she asked with ice in her tone.

Logan was taken aback by her tone. "No. Why?"

She frowned at him. "You sounded… frustrated."

"Only because I'm starving." He held up the take out boxes. "I have enough for both of us. Can I take you home, feed you, and make sure everything's okay with that ankle before I head home?"

"She's going to stay off it completely for the next two weeks," Levi said. "I suspect a hairline fracture. With my healing magic, she won't even need a cast as long as she doesn't aggravate it."

"For two weeks?" he asked.

Levi nodded. "She should go see the Whipple's when they get back in town, but that's the only place she should venture out to. No walking for two weeks. No limping. No nothing. You might want to find someone to stay with her for a couple of weeks, because if she breaks the rules and her foot gets worse, she'll likely need surgery. Got it?"

"Got it." Logan nodded.

"Good. Now I'm headed back to the music shop before the masses try to bang down the door."

Logan glanced over his shoulder at the shop. It was dark, and there wasn't a soul to be found lingering outside. There was hardly a reason to rush, but Logan didn't question him. He had to figure out a way to convince Georgia to move in with him for two weeks. And something told him the gorgeous woman would fight his request tooth and nail. A smile tugged at his lips. He always did love a good challenge.

CHAPTER 5

*G*eorgia stared at the unopened pizza box from her place on her couch and wondered what in the hell was happening to her. She'd been in a state of shock ever since Logan had come to her rescue after she'd fallen and hurt her ankle. It wasn't from the pain either.

Just how was it possible that not one, but *two* scenes she'd written had come true? Had she somehow manifested the events into the universe? It was a terrifying thought. What if she wrote something tragic in her next scene? Would that come true as well? Her blood ran cold. How would she ever finish another book when she'd be second-guessing everything she wrote?

Logan placed a glass of tea in front of her and opened the pizza box. After putting two slices on a paper plate, he handed it to her along with a napkin. "There's salad too if you want some."

"No, thanks. This is more than enough." Georgia took the plate, but just rested it on her lap as her thoughts spun out of control. Was this some sort of delayed family curse? Her fingers itched to pick up her phone and dial her aunt, the only family she had left. But she didn't want to talk about her dilemma in front of Logan. If she was already half convinced that she was going crazy, who knew what he might think of her theory?

"You should eat something," Logan said, taking a seat on the chair to her left.

She glanced at him and blinked. "What?"

He raised one eyebrow and gestured to the plate on her lap. "The pizza? Levi said you'd be weak after the magic he used on your ankle. You need the calories."

"Right." Levi had said she'd likely be ravenous over the next few days while her ankle healed. But currently her stomach was in knots, and the thought of eating was unappealing at best. Still, she picked up a slice and made a show of taking a bite.

Logan smiled at her and dug in to his own meal.

Georgia managed to eat one of the slices, but that was more than enough with all the dread churning around in her gut. Not only was she writing the future, but now she was supposed to stay off her foot for two weeks. How was she going to get around her house or up the stairs to her bedroom? She supposed she could sleep on the couch for a while, but that would get uncomfortable really fast. She let out a groan and pressed her hand to her forehead, trying to ward off her headache.

"It'll be all right," Logan said.

She nodded. "Eventually. I just have to find a way to move around down here for the foreseeable future. Maybe see if I can get groceries and meals delivered. The hardest part will be that I'm homebound. I'm not good at staying home."

"What if you didn't have to?" he asked as he collected their paper dishes and tucked them into a garbage bag.

"What does that mean?" she asked, her brow furrowing in confusion. "Are you going to come pick me up every day and take me to the park or something?"

He laughed. "That wasn't my plan, but it can be arranged if that's what you need."

Georgia narrowed her eyes, wondering what in the world this man was doing in her living room. He'd already done more than anyone could reasonably expect from an acquaintance. She appreciated everything, but surely he had to get back to his own work, right? "Logan, listen. I really appreciate everything you've done for me today, but you really don't need to stay. I'm okay here. I don't want to keep you from your work. Surely you have a deadline to meet, right?"

"Not really." He moved to sit on the coffee table in front of her. "I haven't set a release date yet for my next novel. It can wait a few weeks."

"Weeks? Sounds nice. I almost never get to take that much time off." She gave him a deprecating smile. "My boss is a real witch."

His gaze swept over her, and there was interest there, maybe even a little wolf-like hunger.

Georgia almost snorted when she thought of Faith's comment about not minding if a sexy shifter rescued her, but she managed to keep her dignity even if she did flush from the heat of his gaze.

"Georgia, you're going to need someone to stay with you while you recover. You know that, right?" he asked.

She shrugged. "I'll be fine." She waved a hand dismissively even though she was already wondering how she was going to get around her house without putting any weight on her foot.

33

She didn't even have crutches yet. Someone was going to need to head to Eureka to find some since the healer's office in Keating Hollow was closed. "I'm sure my friends can stop by to check on me periodically."

He shook his head and crossed his arms over his chest. "No way am I leaving you here by yourself. I'll stay."

"Here?" she squeaked out.

"Yeah, here." He glanced around, his gaze landing on the stairs. "It's either that, or I can take you home to my place for a couple of weeks."

"No. That's not necessary," she insisted, internally grimacing at the idea of staying anywhere other than her own place while she was recovering. "I appreciate your offer, but I really think I can handle it."

"Really? How will you get upstairs?" he asked.

"I'll sleep down here." She patted the couch and forced a smile.

"And to the bathroom or kitchen?"

She hid a scowl. "By tomorrow I'll have crutches. I'm sure Hanna or one of my other friends will come help me with anything I need, but honestly, I'm really not high maintenance."

"I didn't think you were." He glanced at the kitchen, looking skeptical. "I just can't see you doing dishes or even making yourself a cup of coffee on crutches without risking your ankle."

"I don't need to do dishes if I just have takeout," she said sweetly.

"Uh-huh. Still, I'm not leaving you alone until you at least have crutches and I can see for myself that you can get around," he said stubbornly.

"You can't just stay here without my consent," she said,

starting to get irritated. Georgia didn't care for being ordered around, especially not by some man she'd just met, no matter how sexy he was when he was being overprotective and bossy. For the love of everything magical, why was that such a turn on? She clearly needed help.

"No. I wouldn't stay if you're absolutely against it, but I would call you every ten minutes just to check in."

Georgia rolled her eyes. "I think you might be exaggerating a bit."

Logan shook his head as his silver eyes glinted with amusement. "I'm not. Like I said, I have some time before I have to start this next book. What else do I have to do besides make sure my new friend isn't trapped on her couch for sixteen hours straight?"

"I never would have guessed that you'd be this annoying," Georgia said with a chuckle. "But even I can see that you're not going to let this go. How about we make a deal? If I can get one of my girlfriends to stay with me, you'll go back to your writing cave and not call to check on me until tomorrow morning. If I can't, I'll let you carry me upstairs and you'll only come up if I text you for help. Deal?"

"Will you answer if I text to check on you?" he asked, already grinning at his victory.

"Only if you keep the texts to a minimum. No more than one before my bedtime at ten and then not again until after eight in the morning."

"Two before ten," he countered.

Georgia burst out laughing at the absurdity of their negotiations. "Fine. But it won't matter because I'm sure I can rustle up one of my friends for a sleepover."

"Sure," he said, standing and moving toward the kitchen.

"I'll get you that herbal tea Levi suggested while you make your calls."

She smirked at the skepticism in his tone. While Georgia was relatively new in town, she did have a great little group of friends who she knew she could absolutely count on.

Ten minutes later, Georgia was scowling and muttering under her breath, *famous last words*. While it was true that she had wonderful friends, they were also very busy with their own lives. She'd already known Amelia was a longshot. It wasn't exactly easy for a new mom to pack up herself and her infant daughter to have a sleepover. And it was impossible when the baby had a slight fever and had been crying nonstop for the past two hours. Needless to say, the pair were staying home while Grayson took care of them. Hanna was in Christmas Grove with Rhys for a short getaway. Miranda was out of town. Faith didn't even answer her phone, and when Georgia called Yvette, she learned that Faith was having nighttime morning sickness and that she was probably asleep.

Yvette had offered to come over but warned her that she'd have to bring Skye as Jacob was working late at the bookstore. The screaming from the toddler in the background had already exacerbated Georgia's headache. She just could not bring herself to send away the sweet man in the kitchen so she could replace him with toddler chaos just so her pride wasn't bruised. She'd thanked Yvette for the offer but declined, stating that she didn't want to uproot Skye for the night. After she ended the call, she put her phone down and sighed before calling, "Logan?"

He poked his head around the corner. "Yeah?"

"Looks like you're stuck with me for the night."

His lips curved into a slow, satisfied smile.

Georgia mentally berated herself for the R-rated thoughts

that went through her head when he smiled at her like that. She needed to snap out of it, and the only way to do that was to put some distance between them. "Any chance you could carry me upstairs? I'd like to try to get some words in before I pass out for the evening." As soon as the words were out of her mouth, she wished she could stuff them back in. Had she really just asked him to carry her upstairs right after she'd been thinking they needed distance? What was wrong with her? "Um, or maybe you could just help me to the kitchen. I could write at the table."

"If you want to go upstairs, I'm happy to get you up there," Logan said. "Besides, it will probably be more comfortable elevating your ankle while you're in bed."

"True." She quickly did a mental inventory of what her bedroom might look like. Had she tidied up that morning? Were there any unmentionables lying about? She didn't think so. Georgia liked her space tidy. However, there could be a bra or two hanging in her bathroom. She always hung them to dry and wasn't sure if she'd put the last batch away where they belonged.

"Are you ready now?" he asked.

She nodded, not sure she trusted her voice.

The moment he lifted her into his arms, she let out a small contented sigh.

Logan chuckled softly and then carefully carried her up the stairs to her bedroom.

CHAPTER 6

$\mathcal{N}$ow that Logan wasn't worried about getting Georgia out of the woods and to a healer, he was in no hurry for her to leave his arms. He'd gladly stand next to her bed while she pressed her head into his shoulder for the next several hours if it meant he didn't need to break their connection. She felt that good.

"Logan?" she asked, tilting her head up. "Are you waiting for someone to fluff the pillows?"

"Yes," he said as if he were deadly serious.

She shook her head, mildly exasperated.

Damn, he loved provoking her.

Georgia pressed her fingers to his ribs and poked.

"Hey!" he jumped back, jostling her, and tightened his hold when he feared he might drop her.

"Well, that wasn't quite what I was going for," she said breathlessly, her lips mere inches from his.

He stared down at her pouty mouth, desperate to taste her. His entire body craved her with a fierceness that nearly made him lose his mind. Had he ever wanted to kiss someone as much as he wanted to kiss Georgia in that moment?

No. Never.

"Logan," she whispered, and when he met her gaze, the desire there was unmistakable.

He moved in, unable to resist any longer, but before he could brush his lips over hers, his phone started blaring the theme music from *Jaws*, startling him out of the spell that had overtaken them. "Shit," he muttered. "I have to get that."

"*Jaws?*" she asked incredulously. "Whose ringtone is that? Your investment banker?"

He snorted with laughter and shook his head. "No. It's my brother. It's his favorite movie." Logan set Georgia on her bed carefully, and even grabbed a pillow to elevate her ankle before he finally answered the call. "Seth, what's up?"

"What took you so long? Did you finally find a girl who'll spend more than twenty minutes with you before she dies of boredom?" Seth asked, his tone full of humor.

"Neither science fiction nor fantasy are boring, little brother," Logan said, all too willing to have the same argument about his genre choices that they'd had for as long as Logan could remember. However, there were more important things to worry about. Instead of waiting for the banter they usually engaged in, he dove right in. "How'd it go today?"

"Uh, not quite as planned." All the humor had vanished, and Seth sounded more tired than anything else. "The band is taking a break."

Logan frowned. "What? How? Don't you have tour dates booked?"

"We did, but Cal is claiming he hurt his vocal cords and that his doctor demanded he rest for at least a few months before he can sing again. Without him, there's no show."

"Damn. That sucks. Is it true about his vocal cords?" Logan asked, already knowing the answer.

"No," Seth growled in frustration. "But he's gotten a doctor to sign on to his excuse, so there's really nothing I can do about it."

"You could talk to him," Logan said.

"I tried. It didn't go well. Listen, Logan, how do you feel about having a visitor for a few weeks?"

"You're coming to Keating Hollow?" Logan's lips split into a grin. It had been over a year since he'd seen his brother in person. "When?"

"Now. I'm sitting on your front step."

"Seriously?" Logan glanced at Georgia and found her watching him with interested eyes. He glanced at her ankle and bit back a curse. He didn't want to leave her, but he also needed to go let his brother into his house.

"Seriously. As soon as Cal walked out of the meeting this morning, I got on a plane and came here. I just couldn't deal with staying in that apartment for one more moment. I hope you don't mind."

"Not at all. I'll be there in about ten minutes." He ended the call and gave Georgia an apologetic look.

"Looks like I'll be on my own after all," she said, forcing a smile. "Don't worry about me. I'll manage."

"I'm not leaving you on your own. Or at least not for long," he insisted. "I need to go let my brother into my house and get him settled, and then I'll come right back. He's had a rough couple of weeks."

Georgia reached out and squeezed his hand. "You should stay with him then. I'm fine. The ankle doesn't even really hurt anymore. Levi's magic fingers really did the trick."

Logan shook his head. "Sorry. You're not getting rid of me

that easily. My brother is a grown man. He can take care of himself. I'd just rather he not break a window or pick a lock to get out of the cold. I won't be long. Need anything before I go?"

She waved at a desk near the window. "Just my laptop and my notebook. My work in progress could really use some attention if I plan on keeping my next editing date."

"On it." Logan retrieved her laptop and the notebook she requested. Then he went downstairs and made her a fresh mug of tea and grabbed a bag of cookies and a bottle of water before heading back upstairs. He placed everything on her nightstand and said, "While I'm out, I'll get my brother to go with me to get your car. Is there anything else you need?"

She paused for a moment then glanced down as she said, "Thank you. You're very kind. The keys are in the pocket of my jacket near the front door." When she looked up, she glanced at the drinks and cookies. "That looks like every writer's survival pack. Tea, water, and cookies? The only thing missing is the chocolate."

He gave her a half smile and pulled a Twix bar out of his back pocket. "I'd planned on eating this when I got to the end of my hike, but lucky for you, I got sidetracked." He placed the candy on the table with her cookies and then stood back, resisting the urge to kiss her. That moment had passed. "Call or text me if you need anything while I'm gone, okay?"

She rolled her eyes. "I'm fine, Logan. Go tend to your brother. I'll have my hands full as I work out the next chapter. As I always say, the two hardest scenes to write are fight scenes and sex scenes."

He raised one interested eyebrow. "Which one is it this time?"

She raised her dark gaze to his and said, "It was supposed to be a fight scene, but now I'm thinking all that build up was probably sexual tension."

Logan swallowed hard, and then with a nod, he turned on his heel and vanished down the stairs.

Less than ten minutes later, he pulled into the driveway of the home he'd purchased a few months before. It was just on the outskirts of Keating Hollow, above the river with a view of the mountains. There were a handful of houses nearby, giving him a few neighbors, but they were divided by an acre or two, giving each household plenty of privacy. After living in cities his entire life, it was a welcome and needed change.

When he'd first visited Keating Hollow, he'd found a peace he hadn't ever known. Not even when he'd visited small towns up and down the west coast or the little villages in Maine and Vermont. He'd thought he was destined to be restless forever, moving around all the time, looking for something that didn't exist. He'd unexpectantly found it in this small magical town that looked more like an enchanted Hallmark set than an actual place where people lived.

He'd found his place. And every time he came home to his cabin on the hill, everything inside of him settled. But this time as he stepped out of his SUV, his chest tightened at the sight on his porch. His brother looked defeated and had a sadness etched around his eyes that made Logan want to throttle Calvin Bishop. The man had all but ripped Seth's heart out, and now he was tanking their band, all because he was a selfish asshole.

Logan strode over to his brother, offered him his hand, and pulled him up into a bear hug. "It's good to see you, man."

"You, too," Seth choked out.

They held on for a long moment until Seth finally stepped back and cleared his throat. "Thanks for coming. It's getting cold out."

Logan nodded, unlocked his front door, and hauled Seth's suitcase into the small foyer. "Not a problem at all. But I could use your help with something if you don't have anything pressing to do."

Seth laughed. "Already making me work for my lodging?"

"Yep. No free rides around here," he teased. "I just need to go pick up a friend's car and get it back to their house. Need someone to take me though. You up for a short ride?" If he was out and about, he might as well make good on his promise to Georgia to take care of her vehicle for her.

"Sure. Just point me to a restroom first."

Logan pointed down the hall and made his way into the kitchen where he fixed them both a cup of coffee. By the time Seth returned, Logan was waiting near the front door with two travel mugs. "Here." He handed one to Seth and led the way back outside.

"Thanks, brother," Seth said as he climbed into the passenger seat. "How'd you know I needed this?"

"You look like you haven't slept in a month," Logan said. "A weekend at the spa probably couldn't cure those dark circles under your eyes."

Seth groaned. "Thanks a lot, princess. Not all of us have the luxury of sleeping in until noon."

Logan grinned at him. "I'd rather sleep than deal with groupies."

"You and me both," Seth muttered and took another long sip of the hot coffee.

"Liar," Logan said with a wink. He knew his brother lived

for his music. Though after the past few months he'd had, Logan was certain he could use a nice long break.

"We'll see." Seth turned his dark blue eyes on his older brother. "Now, tell me about this friend of yours. Why are you picking up her car for her?"

"How do you know it's a her?" Logan asked, knowing he wasn't going to be able to stall for long.

"Seriously?" His brother gave him an incredulous look. "Don't bullshit me. Whoever she is, you like her. A lot."

"Stop. It isn't like that. We're just friends." While it was the truth, it wasn't exactly the *whole* truth. There was a lot more than friendship sparking between them.

"Whatever you say, brother," Seth said, shaking his head. "Since you don't want to talk about your mystery woman, tell me about your latest book. How's it going?"

"It's not. Not yet anyway. I haven't started it." Logan made the turn down the dirt road that led to the trailhead where they'd left Georgia's car.

"So, you're just hanging out with your 'friend' and doing favors for her?" Seth asked with an air of innocence.

"No. I do other things," Logan said defensively.

"Like what?" Seth turned to stare Logan down as they pulled to a stop next to Georgia's silver Audi.

Logan scrambled to come up with something other than his daily hikes, and without thinking, he said, "I sat in on a jam session with some guys from town."

Seth's eyes widened. "You played the guitar?"

Dammit. Logan frowned, mentally kicking himself for saying anything about playing again. His brother would see through any lie, even one of omission.

"You did, didn't you?" Seth asked, awe in his tone. "You're really playing again?"

"Fine. Yes, I played during the jam session, and I helped a friend out when the karaoke sound system failed while she was singing at the brewery. It's no big deal."

Seth shook his head in amazement. "She must be something special to get you back on your guitar."

"Let it go, Seth."

"If you say so. But I just have to say this one thing, and then I'll drop it."

Logan sighed. "Fine. Spit it out."

Seth stared his brother in the eye. "It's long past time you opened your heart again."

"No, it's not," Logan shot back. "And you know why."

"You can't keep shutting everyone out," Seth said with a sigh. "You deserve love in your life. You can't keep blaming yourself."

Logan shook his head and climbed out of his SUV. Without saying another word, he unlocked Georgia's car and slipped into the driver's seat.

As Seth hopped out of the SUV, he called, "You're *not* cursed, Logan. Sometimes bad things just happen. Stop punishing yourself."

Gritting his teeth, he started Georgia's car and backed out of the space.

Seth walked over to the window and waved his hand, indicating for Logan to lower it.

"I'm not talking about this," Logan said, staring straight ahead.

"All right. I just wanted to know when you'd be back to the house."

Logan turned to look at him. "No idea. Text if you need anything."

"I'll manage," Seth said.

"I have no doubt you will." When his brother took a step back, Logan sped out of the parking lot, leaving a cloud of dust in his rearview mirror.

CHAPTER 7

*A*s soon as Georgia heard her door slam and the hum of Logan's SUV fade off into the distance, she grabbed her phone and called her Aunt Dee. Her palms started to sweat while she waited for her favorite person to answer her call.

"Hey, baby. It's about time I heard from you. How long's it been? Three? Four weeks?" her aunt said by way of greeting.

Guilt crawled up Georgia's spine. It really had been too long since she'd touched base with her aunt. "I'm sorry, Auntie Dee. I've been buried in a new book. You know how I get sometimes."

"Oh, I know. I just miss talking to you. So, tell me everything. How's Keating Hollow treating you? How's the book going? And please tell me you've found some hottie to take you out a couple nights a week."

Georgia shook her head. Her aunt was way too invested in her nonexistent love life. "No one is taking me out a couple nights a week. Keating Hollow is just as wonderful as ever, and I fully expect you to come visit me over the holidays. As for the book... Well, that's what I'm calling about."

"You need to bounce some plot ideas off me?" she asked excitedly. Aunt Dee loved talking book plotlines. Usually her suggestions were way over the top, and Georgia almost never used them. But often they sparked other ideas that ended up being exactly what Georgia needed to make a story work. Lots of times those chats were invaluable to Georgia.

"No, not today. Actually, I was wondering if you know of any witches in our family line who were seers or spirit witches," Georgia said.

"Sure. Aunt Lenora was a spirit witch. She sometimes had visions. Most of them were very unreliable, though. Like the time she told me I was going to marry a fireman and move to the beach."

Georgia frowned. "You *did* marry a fireman and move to the beach."

"Uh-huh. But he was fired two months after we were married and then ran off with that floozy from Mr. Richard's Midnight Revue. Three weeks later, I was evicted and had to move into a one-room studio in downtown LA with Stinky Kate from the diner." She let out a huff of irritation. "It most definitely wasn't the happy ending she promised."

"No, it doesn't sound like it." But still, the vision had been correct. "What happened to your aunt Lenora? Did she keep having visions?"

"Yep. Lots of them. Most were stuff like what would come in the mail or if it would rain that day. I never believed those because so much of it was too easy to predict. It's not hard to know the electric bill is going to arrive on the same day every month or predict rain when the sky is full of dark rain clouds. You know?"

"Yeah, that would make me skeptical, too," Georgia agreed. She relaxed against her headboard and waited out her aunt, knowing she wasn't nearly done spilling the tea about her relative.

"But don't go thinking she wasn't a powerful seer," Dee warned.

"I wouldn't dream of it."

"Damn straight. Because Aunt Lenora proved to be the hero of Cricket Moon Landing. She's the one who had the vision of little Henry Vernon sleeping in the Frederick's barn when it went up in flames because of shoddy wiring. If she hadn't called the sheriff right away, there would have been a tragedy that day. Instead, little Henry grew up to be a firefighter who singlehandedly saved Aunt Lenora's house when it caught fire due to a wildfire that sent burning embers onto her roof."

"Wow, talk about full circle," Georgia said. "Amazing how that all worked out."

"Aunt Lenora was an angel even when some people were skeptical of her talents. She just kept warning people if they needed a warning and dismissed the naysayers. Honestly, she was badass. I hope I got just a fraction of her moxie."

"No doubt about it. You have more moxie than anyone else I know," Georgia said, meaning it. Her aunt Dee had a spark that was blinding at times.

"Thank you, my dear. But now you need to tell me why you asked about seers and spirit witches." Her tone turned serious when she asked, "Have you had a vision?"

"Sort of but not exactly." Georgia sucked in a breath. "It's more like I willed events into existence."

"You mean like on purpose? You didn't try to cast any spells did you?" There was no mistaking the judgment in her tone.

"No. Nothing like that. You know I don't have magic. Or at least I thought I didn't," Georgia said. "I started a new book recently, and some of the scenes I've written have played out in real life."

"What does that mean? You wrote a scene, and then what? You saw it in the news or something?"

"Or something," Georgia admitted. "They happened to me." She went on to describe the two scenes she'd written that were mirrored by her interactions with Logan. "I'm afraid I'm unconsciously willing these events to happen. Is that possible?"

There was silence on the other end of the line.

Georgia waited a few beats before asking, "Aunt Dee? You still there?"

"I'm here, baby. Just thinking. I've never heard of anyone willing something into existence without a very strong spell or potion. Since you're not doing that, I doubt that's what's happening."

"But I'm writing them down, and then they're actually happening. To me. Are you sure I'm not forcing these events? What happens if I write a scene where someone dies? Or gets sick? Or does something unforgiveable? Will it be my fault? How am I ever going to write another book?" Georgia was panicking now, and her pulse was racing.

"Georgia," Dee said. "Listen, I know how you must feel, but I strongly believe that you probably aren't responsible for these events. I'd guess it's more likely that you're seeing the event in your mind and then writing about it. So likely, it would've happened whether you wrote about it or not."

"Probably? Likely? Neither of those words are instilling the kind of confidence I need to finish this book. How can I keep writing this when I could be influencing people and events? What if I write a love scene and then end up in bed with someone against their will?" The very idea of that scenario made her stomach turn. "I can't write a romance without the romance!"

Dee chuckled. Actually chuckled. For the first time in memory, Georgia wanted to yell at her aunt and demand to know what exactly she thought was so funny. Instead, she gritted her teeth and said, "It's getting late. I should go and get some rest."

"Oh, honey. I'm sorry. I can tell you're irritated with me. It was just that I think you're reading way too much into this. Even if you *are* writing events into action, I strongly feel that you'd never end up in bed with someone who didn't want to be there, and I say that with one thousand percent certainty."

"Well, yeah. But at this point, I'm afraid to even leave the house if I'm going to be acting out some of the stuff I've written." Not that she had to leave the house to see Logan. No doubt he'd be back in just a few minutes. "The last thing I need is for a wolf shifter to show up and bite me so that I'm bound to him."

"Do you think that ever really happens?" Dee asked wistfully. "I could really use some growly action to liven things up over here."

"Aunt Dee! Come on. Be serious."

"Fine. Here's serious for you. If you're really worried that you're manifesting these events, go find an herbalist. Have her concoct something for you that would inhibit that particular power. Then go home and write the sexiest sex scene you can manage."

"Why the sexiest one?" Georgia asked.

"Because if the potion doesn't work, you might as well live your life to the fullest, right?" She snickered. "I mean, if it's going to happen, it should at least be worthwhile."

"You're so wrong," Georgia said, shaking her head. "I can't believe you said that."

"Yes, you can," Dee said. "I've said way worse than that in my day. Now, tell me about this Logan guy and why you haven't jumped his bones yet."

"Forget it. He's just a friend," Georgia insisted.

"Right. And I didn't marry my firefighter because I wanted to sleep with the sexiest man I'd ever met. If I'd let him talk for longer than five minutes, I might have made a different decision. But still, no regrets. That man was so big, I had to—"

"Aunt Dee! Stop," Georgia said with a giggle. "I do not need to know the details of your sex life."

"Sex life?" she said in mock surprise. "I was going to say he was so big I had to special order his suit for our wedding."

"Lies," Georgia said, laughing. "All lies. But congratulations. It sounds like he took you for a real ride before he hightailed it out of town with that floozy."

Aunt Dee let out a soft sigh. "Did he ever. The only part of him I missed was his—"

"Goodnight, Aunt Dee. Love you."

"Love you, too, sweetheart. Be careful with your ankle and call me tomorrow. I'll be dying to know how tonight turned out after your man gets back."

"He's not my man. He's just a friend who's been caught in the crossfire of my writing," Georgia said.

"Yeah. I hear you. I hope you shaved your legs this morning." Dee cackled and added, "Night, doll. Talk soon."

The line went dead, and Georgia tossed the phone down as she let her head thunk back against her headboard. She hadn't gotten any answers, and writing that sex scene was completely out of the question. Maybe her next scene should send the love interest out of town for a long weekend. Then there'd be no danger of compelling Logan to do anything. Well, except for leaving town.

She couldn't do that. His brother had just arrived. And like it or not, she was laid up in bed and needed help. Or she did for at least the next day until she got her crutches. Maybe by then she'd have had time to see the herbalist for a potion to neutralize her newfound magical ability.

For over thirty years, Georgia had thought she'd been short-changed by the magic gene. In her younger days, she'd felt robbed of her birthright. Everyone in her family had magic. Her mom, her aunt, her grandmother. But not Georgia. Or at least not until now. But this felt more like a curse instead of a gift. Is that what her mother had meant when she'd told Georgia that being a witch was just as much of a burden as it was a blessing?

Maybe. She picked up a framed picture from her nightstand and stared at the photo of her and her mother taken just days after Georgia's college graduation. They had their arms around each other and were laughing. It was only a week later when Georgia got the phone call that her mother had suffered a brain aneurysm and was gone just like that. Georgia had been numb for months after that. Not only had she lost her mother, she'd lost her best friend. It had been the worst year of her life, and she still cried if she thought about it too hard.

"What do you think, Mom?" Georgia asked the woman in the picture. "Am I writing stuff I see or making stuff happen by writing it?"

Georgia waited for some sort of answer from the universe, but nothing came, not even the whisper of a hug she usually felt when she talked to her mother. There was just silence.

Georgia wrapped her arms around herself and added, "Miss you more than ever."

The air in the room warmed, and just like that, she felt the hug she craved.

Georgia smiled and relaxed against the headboard. She might not have any answers, but her soul had settled. And that was enough for now.

CHAPTER 8

On his way back to Georgia's, Logan made an impromptu stop at A Spoon Full of Magic. The front window had been decorated with an elaborate edible chocolate fall scene. There was a big white farmhouse at the end of a treelined road with enchanted red and orange leaves rustling in the breeze. The nostalgia soothed him, and he wondered how he'd ever lived in any of the various concrete cities he'd settled in over the years.

The door opened and a woman with curly gray hair poked her head out. "Looking for something in particular?"

He glanced over at the woman with kind eyes and said, "Yes. Got anything that is like an anti-love potion?"

She opened the door wider, stepped out, and studied him for a moment. Her eyes narrowed as she frowned. "I don't think an anti-love potion is what you need. Looks like you've already got walls around that heart of yours. Or is this for someone else?"

Logan gaped at her. "Uh, what?"

"Come on in. We'll see if we can't find something you need." She smiled sweetly and held the door open for him.

For the life of him, he didn't know why he followed her into the store. He should have just jumped back into Georgia's car and taken off, but there was something compelling about the older woman, a wisdom that had him curious to see what she was going to recommend. "Yeah, okay."

The rich scent of expensive chocolate assaulted his senses, making his mouth water. He glanced around at the shelves, taking in the packaged hot chocolates that boasted everything from love potions to antiaging serums. No wonder the shop was so popular. Who wanted to bother with creams or herbal pills when they could suck down delicious hot cocoa?

"It's Logan, isn't it?" the woman asked, holding out her hand. "I'm Miss Maple, owner of A Spoon Full of Magic. It's nice to finally meet you."

Logan shook her hand and smiled at her. "I'm that notorious, am I?"

She shrugged. "We get a fair number of writers around these parts. Word gets around when they're in town. Once you stop by the bookstore and sign copies there, everyone hears about it."

He chuckled. "Small town gossip. It's the same everywhere, isn't it?"

"Not quite the same in Keating Hollow. We protect our own, so you can be sure no one will be pointing tourists to your place or anything like that." She sat at one of the tables and nodded, inviting him to join her.

He sat as if compelled, and he wondered if Miss Maple was using a minor compelling spell because this entire interaction was completely out of the norm for him.

"Now, tell me what you're looking for," Miss Maple said.

Her hazel eyes were kind as she waited patiently for him to speak.

"Just something to take to Georgia. She hurt her ankle today, and I wanted to get her something just to raise her spirits a little."

She nodded thoughtfully. "What about you? You did ask me for an anti-love potion. Are you actively trying not to fall for... someone?"

He cleared his throat. "Yeah, I guess you could say that. I'm not really built for relationships."

The older woman pressed her lips together into a thin line. "That's not what I see at all. Your aura suggests you're as loyal as the earth is deep. Loyal people tend to be the most committed."

Logan shifted in his chair, more than a little uncomfortable with their conversation, but still, he couldn't seem to find the will to stand and walk away. "I've already met and lost my soul mate. It doesn't happen twice."

"Are you sure about that?" Miss Maple stood and wandered behind the counter. After rustling around in a cabinet, she returned to Logan's table and handed him two packages. "The red one is for your lady. The white one is for you."

"What are they?"

She smiled softly. "The red one will help Georgia relax. I'm sure she needs it. The white one is for you, and it helps with clarity. If you're feeling unsure or confused, it will help strip away anything that is clouding your judgment. It will make it easier to focus on what you truly want and need."

He frowned. "It sounds more like an herb to make me forget my convictions."

"Forget?" She shook her head and smiled warmly at him.

"No. Like I said, it's to help with clarity. You don't have to eat it, but it's there if you want it."

Logan was certain he was being played by Miss Maple, but he still couldn't bring himself to say no. She must have been putting some low-level magic into the air, because he wasn't acting himself at all. He hadn't ever purchased potions or herb infused edibles that could alter his mind. Still, he pulled out his wallet and said, "How much do I owe you?"

Miss Maple patted his hand. "It's on the house. Please tell Georgia I'm sorry about her ankle and I look forward to seeing her as soon as she's up and around again."

"Yeah, okay," Logan said. "I will."

Miss Maple put the chocolates into a bag and asked, "Can I get you a couple of hot chocolates before you go?"

"Only if you let me pay for them," he insisted.

"Deal." Miss Maple hustled behind the counter and whipped up two hot chocolates, complete with real whipped cream. After Logan paid and tipped generously, she walked him to the door. "Good night, Logan. It was wonderful to finally meet you."

"You, too, Miss Maple. I've heard all about your wonderful treats at the farmers' market. I'll have to stop by your booth next time."

"Please do. I'd love that." She opened the door and walked out onto the cobbled sidewalk, locking up behind them. "Drive safely," she said and then walked down the street, disappearing around a corner before Logan could even slip into the car.

As he drove back toward Georgia's house, he was preoccupied with his encounter with the shop owner. She felt like the grandmother he'd never had, and even though he was certain he'd been affected by her magic, he liked her and wouldn't mind spending more time with her. Maybe she was exactly what he needed. Someone to talk to about anything and everything even if he never followed her advice.

Logan shook his head and let out a bark of laughter. It just figured that besides Georgia, the person he was most interested in befriending was a grandmotherly type who owned a chocolate shop.

He was still chuckling when he came to a stop sign at the end of Main Street. After pausing, he pressed onto the gas and immediately slammed on the brakes when a car came out of nowhere. The brakes squealed and the car jerked to a stop, but not before he clipped the back fender of the black convertible.

Logan's heart hammered against his ribcage as he sat there for a moment, shaken up that he hadn't seen the other vehicle until it was too late.

The car door flew open, and a tall, dark-haired man climbed out. He stalked to the back of his car to study the damage before making his way back toward Logan.

Grabbing his phone off the passenger seat, Logan exited the car. "Hey, man. I'm really sorry about that. I didn't see you until it was too late."

"If you'd made a complete stop, maybe you'd have had more time to check out the intersection before you clipped my tail," he said coldly. Then he eyed Logan's phone. "Looks like you were busy doing something other than driving."

"What?" Logan stood taller, more than a little irritated at the man's tone. "I wasn't talking on the phone. I grabbed it so we can call the town sheriff to make an accident report."

"Sure, you did." He pulled his phone out of his back pocket and made a call. Before Logan could look up the number to the town's sheriff's office, the man said, "Yes. I need to make an accident report."

Logan put his phone away and walked over to assess the

damage. The BMW had suffered a broken tail light and some minor damage to the fender. To his surprise, the only damage to Georgia's car was a dent in the left side of the bumper. Score one for the Audi, zero for the BMW.

It wasn't long before he spotted the patrol car making its way toward them. Logan got out his driver's license and his insurance card. After writing down his insurance information and contact number on the back of a business card, he handed it to the other man who was pacing on the side of the road. "Here. I have excellent insurance. Don't worry about a thing."

"So you're admitting you're at fault?" the other man asked.

Logan shrugged. "I'm not sure. Did you stop at your stop sign?"

"Yes," the BMW driver insisted.

"Then I guess that's your answer." Logan was pretty positive he was at fault, but he wasn't going to admit to anything. That was for the police and the insurance people to figure out.

"It's not—" The man paused mid-sentence as he stared at the card. "You're Logan Malone?"

"That's what it says on my birth certificate," Logan said.

"The *author* Logan Malone?" he asked.

Logan was uncomfortable with confirming his identity even though it would take the man less than five minutes to work it out if he googled him. He was just always uncomfortable talking to people about his profession unless it was another author. He didn't deal well with feeling like a minor celebrity. Not after his experience with his band. These days he was more than happy to release books and then sit in the background to let them speak for themselves.

A car door slammed, and boots echoed off the asphalt as

the sheriff's deputy made his way to them. "Looks like a minor fender bender," the police officer said. "Anyone hurt?"

"No, we're fine," Logan volunteered. "It's exactly what it looks like."

The officer glanced at the other man. "How about you sir?"

"I'm fine. My BMW isn't."

"I can see that." The officer took a look at the two cars then got to work filling out the paperwork. When he was done, he said, "You can pick up copies of this at the office sometime tomorrow after we get it typed up."

"Thanks, officer…?" Logan started.

"It's Deputy Baker. Or Drew." He held out a hand to Logan. "It's nice to meet you, finally. I heard from my sister-in-law Yvette that we had another author in town."

"It's nice to meet you, too, Drew. Hopefully we meet under better circumstances next time," Logan said.

"Yeah, I bet Georgia isn't going to be too happy when you tell her she needs a new bumper." Drew tapped his pen on his clipboard. "Though I suppose it could be worse."

"Much worse," Logan agreed. "Hopefully the cocoa from A Spoon Full of Magic will help smooth things over."

"Doesn't hurt." Drew nodded toward the other man and said, "Goodnight, Mr. Steele. Enjoy the rest of your stay here in Keating Hollow."

"Call me Austin," Mr. Steele said. "It wasn't the way I wanted to start my stay here, but I appreciate your quick attention to the matter."

Drew dipped his head, acknowledging the other man, and then he took off in his patrol car, leaving the two men standing there.

"Well, I guess if you give me your information, we'll be all done here," Logan said.

"Right." Austin jotted down his information and handed it to Logan.

"Thanks, man. And really, I'm sorry about your car." He moved to get into the Audi but paused when the other man spoke.

"Do you know Gideon Alexander?" Austin asked.

Logan paused, staring the other man down. Everyone in town knew Gideon. He was a former Hollywood bigwig, turned artist who'd made a quiet life from himself in Keating Hollow with a fellow writer Miranda Moon. What did this stranger want with him? Logan had no idea, but without knowing anything about him, there was no chance Logan would tell him anything. Besides, it wasn't hard to find Gideon. He owned the local art gallery. If this man wanted to talk to him, he could find him there after a simple internet search. "Can't say as I do," he lied and then got into the Audi without another word. He had cocoa to deliver.

CHAPTER 9

*G*eorgia stared at the clock on her nightstand and wondered when Logan would return. Or had he changed his mind and decided to stay home with his brother? It was what he should do. However, if she was honest with herself, she not only needed the help, she wanted him there.

Why had she resisted him so much when she had no one who could come stay with her? She knew why. Georgia was a proud woman who hated the idea of being dependent on anyone, much less a man she was attracted to. Why couldn't she be graceful and effortless? No, instead she was the klutz who'd fallen on a trail and had to be rescued. If she were writing the book, the heroine definitely would have found a way to walk out of the woods.

But this was real life, and she couldn't control the plotline like she did in her books.

Sighing to herself, she opened her laptop and got to work on ideas for the next scene. She needed to find a way for the couple to come together. Something to ignite that spark between them.

She couldn't help thinking about the last few interactions she'd had with Logan, and from there an idea formed. Her fingers flew across the keyboard as she jotted down a few notes about the heroine learning to play the guitar. Of course, the hero would be her teacher, and after the hero placed his hands over hers to help her master a particularly rough series of notes, they'd kiss for the first time.

Georgia had taken a few lessons over at Magical Notes, so at least she'd know what she was talking about when she wrote that scene. She eyed her guitar case that was leaning against the wall a few feet from her bed. She scooted over, reached out, and snagged the case. If she was going to write a musical scene, she wanted to feel the strings under her fingers in order to help her submerge herself when it came time to get busy typing.

After settling against her headboard with her left leg bent and the other stretched out in front of her, Georgia pulled the guitar into her lap. The instrument still felt unfamiliar in her grip, and she took some time to position it so that she was comfortable. Then she let her fingers strum over the strings.

The sound of the guitar always soothed her, even when she was just messing around. Georgia played a few simple chords and smiled to herself. Her fingers were clumsy, but she didn't care. For her, the joy was in the act of playing, producing something other than words. Something just for her.

"Hey," Logan said softly from her doorway. "I didn't know you played."

She quickly put the guitar to the side, embarrassed by her near nonexistent skill level. "I don't. Not really. I started taking lessons a few weeks ago. Just for fun." She let out a self-conscious bark of laughter. "I barely know where to position my fingers."

"You were doing fine." He smiled and walked over to an armchair near her window that faced the back of her home. When he turned around, the smile was gone. "I have some news."

Georgia stiffened. This was where he was going to tell her he couldn't stay over. Her heartbeat quickened, and a ball of anxiety started to form in her gut.

Calm the hell down, Georgia, she berated herself. *You'll survive one night until you can get some damned crutches.*

"Okay. Do you need to go spend the evening with your brother? Is everything okay?" she asked.

"I'm not going anywhere. Not unless you tell me to get out." He forced a small smile. "My brother is going through some stuff in his professional and personal life, but he'll be all right. No, this is about your car."

She blinked. "What's wrong with my car? Did you have problems with one of the tires? I just had one fixed after I ran over a nail. I knew I should have replaced it instead."

"It's not the tire. I had a small accident."

Her eyes widened and she opened her mouth to say something, but he put his hand up, stopping her.

"No one was hurt, and it's just a minor fender bender," he said. "Your bumper needs repaired or replaced. My insurance will take care of everything, or if for some reason they don't cover it, I'll do it myself. The other car needs a new taillight and repairs to his fender."

All the tension drained out of her. "Oh. Well, that's too bad. But accidents happen, and no one was hurt." She shrugged. It sucked that she'd have to deal with a repair, but Georgia had never had an emotional connection to any of her vehicles. If it could be fixed, it really wasn't a big deal. "It's just a car."

"You're not upset?" he asked, seemingly surprised by her attitude.

"No. Not unless you were texting and driving or something equally as stupid." She peered at him. "You weren't, were you?"

He chuckled and shook his head. "Nope. I just didn't see the other car until it was too late."

She lifted one shoulder. "As long as no one was hurt, that's all I care about."

"No one was hurt," he assured her. Then he handed her the package from A Spoon Full of Magic. "I got you something."

"A bribe to get me to not be angry about the car accident?" she asked, holding the package up and raising one eyebrow. Her lips twitched in amusement as she added, "A bigger box of chocolates would've been more appropriate for an apology."

His eyes glinted with humor as he shook his head. "I'll remember that next time. Miss Maple picked it out for you. It's infused with herbs and is supposed to help you relax." Logan crossed the room and picked up a paper cup he'd left on a small table near her bedroom door. "I also got us some hot cocoa. Hope you're up for a sugar fix."

"Always." Georgia held her hand out for the hot cocoa. If there was ever a time that she needed something to help her calm down, it was now. Ever since Logan had walked back into her room, she'd been wound up with tension. At first, it was because of her worries that he'd leave and then about the accident. Now it was because all the rest of her worries had been laid to rest and there was no getting around the fact that he was staying with her. All night.

Georgia's skin broke out in goosebumps when their fingers brushed as he handed her the cocoa. That spark that she'd felt the first day they'd met was still there. And she wanted more than anything for him to sit next to her on the bed instead of in the chair across the room. She quickly unwrapped the treat from Miss Maple and popped the chocolate covered caramel into her mouth. She closed her eyes and let herself savor the yummy goodness.

Logan cleared his throat, and when Georgia opened her eyes, he was holding his own cocoa cup and staring at the floor.

"Everything okay?" she asked.

His cheeks were full of color, and his voice was husky when he looked up at her and said, "Yeah. Sure."

"Good. Now what? We could play cards if you want. Or watch a movie."

He glanced around and frowned. "No television?"

"It's downstairs. You'd have to carry me down there, or we could watch something on my computer." Georgia secretly loved the idea of them sitting close together on her bed watching a movie. It was intimate but innocent enough. As long as she kept her hands to herself.

Logan reached out and picked up her guitar. "I have a better idea. Ever since I heard you sing at the brewery, I've been hoping to hear that lovely tone of yours again." He sat on the edge of the bed and strummed a few chords. "What do you think? Will you be my vocalist?"

"You just want me to sing?" she asked warily, staring at the guitar.

"If you want to." He started plucking the guitar, and it only took her a moment to realize he was playing "Say Something" by Great Big World.

"I've never heard that on anything other than the piano," she said.

He just smiled at her and continued to play.

The music overtook her almost instantly. She didn't know why, but when Logan played, she felt as if she was transfixed, as if magic was penetrating her heart and soul. There wasn't any thought process. She just let herself sink right into the song and felt it all the way to her toes as she started to sing.

The words poured from Georgia as the sweet guitar notes filled the room. Georgia met Logan's intense gaze and sang the heart-wrenching words with everything she had. Those feelings of loss that were never far away roared back, making tears prick her eyes. As she sang the last note of the song, one lone tear rolled down her cheek.

Logan's fingers stilled on the guitar and in the silence that followed, he reached over and tenderly wiped the tear away. She closed her eyes, savoring his touch. When she finally opened them, he was still right there.

Georgia cleared her throat, and Logan moved back, putting space between them.

"That was... beautiful," she said, her voice a little unsteady.

Logan put the guitar aside on the bed and stared at her with awe. "Your voice is incredible."

Georgia's cheeks flushed. "Thank you. I've always enjoyed singing."

"You could've had a soloist career. You know that, right?"

"Me?" She let out a bark of laughter and pulled the guitar into her lap just to have something to do with her hands. "All I've ever really wanted was to be a writer. Singing is just a hobby."

He raised one eyebrow. "Like playing the guitar?"

She smiled, started to strum the strings, and nodded. "Sure. It's just that I know how to sing. I barely know how to position my hands on this thing."

"Want some help?" he asked.

"Help doing what?"

"Playing." He got up and moved to stand next to her. "Face the other way, toward your windows."

Georgia blinked at him, a warning bell going off in her head. She could not let him help her play the guitar, not after she'd written notes that something similar would be the next scene in her book. No. Nope. Absolutely not. "Maybe we should just call it a night."

He frowned. "Really? Oh. Yeah, sure. You're probably tired."

She wasn't, and the idea of playing more music with him was very appealing. Her fingers glided over the strings one more time before she stopped and handed him the instrument. "Thanks for playing for me. I really enjoyed singing along."

Logan put the guitar back into its case and smiled at her as he leaned it against the wall. "Anytime."

Georgia stared at him as he stuffed his hands in his pockets. Neither of them moved, not that Georgia could really go anywhere anyway. But that zap of energy was sparking between them again, and she couldn't help but reach out and take his hand in hers. "Thank you for helping me today. I don't know what would've happened if you hadn't been there."

He squeezed her fingers and joked, "You probably wouldn't have had a dented bumper."

She rolled her eyes. "I'll take a dented bumper over being stranded on a trail for hours without help." They were still holding hands, and Georgia found herself unable to let go.

He eyed their connection and then sat down next to her. His gaze was intense as he brushed her dark curls out of her eyes. "Are you sure you're ready to call it a night?"

Her breath caught. She knew she should say yes. Her head screamed for her to say it, to send him downstairs so that she wouldn't be tempted, but instead, she shook her head and dropped her gaze to his mouth.

His tongue darted out, briefly wetting his lips. The air between them was charged, and when he let out a breath and moved in, she leaned toward him, unable to stop herself. She sighed when his lips brushed over hers.

Electricity sparked, sending shivers all over her body. If she'd thought she had a connection to him before, this was something else entirely. It was as if they were tethered together by an unseen force.

Logan's hand cupped the back of her neck, and she let her eyes flutter closed as she opened for him, desperate for his taste.

It had been far too long since she'd tasted a man, and she drank in the faint traces of sweet cocoa. "Hmm," Georgia murmured and leaned into him, wanting more, *needing* more.

"Damn, I've been wanting to do this ever since I walked back in here tonight," Logan said, tightening his hold on her. "I don't think I've ever wanted anything more."

Georgia's entire body vibrated with the need for him to touch her, and she wanted nothing more than to lay back and pull him on top of her. To feel his body completely pressed against her as she got her fill of him.

But his words... *I've been wanting to do this ever since I walked back in here tonight.* He hadn't wanted to kiss her earlier. It wasn't until after she'd written her notes for that next chapter.

Dammit!

Georgia pulled back and pressed her hand to his chest. "We can't do this."

"What?" He stiffened and dropped his hands, leaving her feeling cold and empty without the connection they shared.

"I'm sorry. I thought…" He stood and took a step back. "It doesn't matter what I thought. I should go."

"Logan," Georgia said, unwilling to end the evening with him thinking she didn't want him. "It's not you. It's me." She sucked in a breath. "It's my fault this is happening."

His frown deepened. "I don't understand. What do you mean it's your fault? I'm the one who kissed you."

She closed her eyes for a brief moment. When she opened them, she blurted, "It's my fault all this is happening. Our meeting, my fractured ankle, you kissing me."

"How can it be your fault?" He sat back down on the edge of the bed.

"I wrote those scenes in my latest book. Then they came true. I can't keep doing this"—she waved a hand between them —"because it's not fair to you."

"I don't get it. How is it unfair to me?"

"Don't you see, Logan?" she asked, raising her voice and wishing she could pace around her room. "I'm writing the scenes, and they're coming true."

He furrowed his brow, clearly confused. "You're acting out the scenes in your book?"

"No!" She covered her face with her hands and let out a groan. She knew she sounded crazy, but she had to make him understand. When she lifted her head, she stared him straight in the eye. "It's magic that's causing you to live the words that I write. That means you're not doing this because you want to; you're doing it because I'm *compelling* you."

CHAPTER 10

*L*ogan wanted to laugh but swallowed the impulse. Georgia was far too earnest and worried about whatever was happening, and he didn't want her to think he wasn't taking her seriously. He wasn't a novice when it came to unusual magic. He knew better than anyone that spirit witches often had unique traits.

"Well, aren't you going to say anything?" she asked, her eyes wide and full of apprehension.

He reached out and brushed his thumb over her cheekbone. "Georgia, I can say with one hundred percent certainty that I'm not doing anything that I don't want to do."

She pressed her lips together into a thin line. "You don't know that. This magic— It's new, and I don't even understand it. But the fact is that I wrote those scenes and then they played out in a way that was far too similar to be a coincidence." She grabbed her laptop and thrust it at him. "Take a look for yourself."

Logan shook his head. "I don't need to. I trust you're telling me the truth."

"Well, then you agree that this is a problem." She crossed her arms over her chest and glared at him.

He couldn't hold the chuckle in that time.

Her eyes narrowed further. "It's not funny. Now I'm afraid to write anything for fear I'm influencing the future."

Logan sobered. "That would be disconcerting. I'm sorry for laughing. It wasn't at you. I promise. It was because I don't have any problems with kissing you. In fact, I want to do it right now. Did you write this scene, too?"

She hesitated and bit her bottom lip. "No, the last notes I made were about the guitar and a first kiss."

"I see." He couldn't keep his gaze from fixating on her mouth. That kiss they'd shared had been one for the record books. The connection between them was electric, and all he wanted was to feel it one more time. "So you've yet to write the second kiss?"

"That's right," she said almost breathlessly.

"So if I kiss you again, it's completely of my own free will, right?"

"Yeah, I guess so." Georgia lifted her hand and brushed a lock of his dark hair off his forehead, and it was then that he noticed all of her apprehension disappear as desire flashed in her dark eyes.

He leaned in, moving slowly so that she had every opportunity to pull back.

Only she didn't. She met him halfway, and when he paused just an inch from her lips, she whispered, "Kiss me, Logan."

"I thought you'd never ask," he said and moved in, covering her mouth with his. That spark shot straight to his chest, lighting him up and making his skin tingle from head to toe. Logan buried his hand in her thick curls and deepened the kiss, getting lost in her as she wrapped her arms around him.

"Georgia," he whispered as he trailed soft kisses down her neck.

She tilted her head back, giving him easier access as she slid her hand under his shirt, trailing her nails over his back.

Everything about her was intoxicating.

But when she laid back on the bed and pulled him so that he was lying on top of her, his head swam and he felt himself being pulled under with some sort of spell. He instinctively knew it wasn't Georgia's magic or anything she'd done. It was another kind of magic. The magic that he'd felt twice before. The kind that crawled into his heart and made him fall head over heels in love with another person.

That could *not* happen. He wouldn't let it.

Logan suddenly stiffened and pulled his head back to stare down at her.

"What's wrong?" she asked, cupping his cheek with her soft palm.

"I..." *Shit. What was he doing?* Logan scrambled off her and put a few feet between himself and the bed. "I'm sorry," he managed to force out. "We shouldn't be doing that. Not now with your ankle. Or when I'm here taking care of you."

"But I didn't write this," she said under her breath. Then her voice strengthened as she added, "Though I should. There's nothing like an interrupted make-out session to frustrate the readers." She let out a humorless laugh. "For the record, Logan, my ankle is fine. Doesn't hurt at all."

"That's good," he said. "I'm very glad to hear that, but we shouldn't do this. Not tonight." *Not ever*, he thought as he tried to find a graceful way to exit the situation. What he really wanted to do was spin on his heel and hightail it out of her house. He wouldn't because he'd already committed to being there to help for the evening, but if it had been any other time, he'd have already been striding down the street, calling his brother to come pick him up.

"Okay," she said, her lips curving down into a small frown.

Was that hurt he saw in her wide eyes. *Dammit!* How could he tell her that he wanted her? *Craved* her even? But there was no way he could get involved with her. Not if there was a possibility of him falling for her. It was too dangerous for both of them.

"I'm sorry, Georgia," he said helplessly as he shoved his hands into the pockets of his jeans. "I should head downstairs. Do you need anything before I go?"

Georgia pushed herself back up on the bed. After straightening her shoulders, her expression was cold when she shook her head. "No, Logan. I'm fine. Goodnight."

He glanced at the en suite bathroom. "Do you need help with… your nightly routine?"

Her eyes flickered to the bathroom, and then she tightened her jaw. "No. But there's a walking stick by my back door. If you can bring that to me, I'll be fine."

"Levi said—" Logan started.

"I know what Levi said. I'll be *fine*."

"Right." The look on her face told him there was nothing he could say that would change her mind about letting him help. Not that he blamed her. There was no way in hell he'd let her help him use the restroom if he was laid up. Especially if she'd just rejected him. "I'll get the walking stick and be right back."

She nodded once, grabbed her laptop, and flipped it open.

As Logan made his way down the stairs, he imagined Georgia writing a murder scene and wondered how much longer he had to live.

A few minutes later, after the walking stick was delivered and Georgia had dismissed him from her presence, Logan was back in the living room, sitting on the edge of the couch with his head in his hands. Images, like a flickering old film, flashed in his mind. The crumpled Mustang. The flashing lights of the ambulance outside the emergency room. Blood staining Cherry's favorite bright yellow dress. And the angry, piercing eyes of Cherry's mother as she blamed him for her death.

The familiar, soul-crushing guilt slammed into him because he knew Cherry's mother was right. Her death was his fault.

The images changed and this time he saw Brit, naked and in bed with Leo Kraven, his tattoos a stark contrast to her alabaster skin. Logan had been so shocked to find them in his bed that he'd stood there for far too long, his eyes wide and his heart shattered in his chest.

Logan flopped back against the couch and squeezed his eyes shut as if that could keep the next image from materializing. He knew it was useless though. Once his mind went down this road, there was no stopping it. His stomach rolled when Brit's lifeless body flashed in his mind. She was lying there on his bathroom floor, a handful of blue pills scattered around her. By the time he'd gotten to her, she was ice cold and her lips were purple. There'd been nothing he could do.

The guilt intensified.

The overdose had happened just two days after he'd told Brit to take her shit and get out. If he'd just gone to that damned therapy appointment she'd asked him to go to, maybe, just maybe it would have made the difference.

Logan stood and shook his head, determined to clear his mind. But he knew that would be impossible. Not after what happened upstairs with Georgia. Or more importantly, after what he'd felt while kissing Georgia.

He'd only ever felt that intense magic with Cherry and Brit.

In both cases, he'd fallen suddenly and very hard. He'd barely known what had hit him.

Both relationships had been intense and all-consuming in their own way. Cherry, the love of his life... His relationship with her had been so full of love that when she'd died, Logan had felt like he'd died right along with her. He'd been a shell of a man, unable to play his guitar, unable to manage his business affairs. Hell, he'd barely been able to get out of bed in the morning.

But then the black cloud over him had started to clear and Brit came into his life. That magic was back, only this time his relationship had been so passionate that he'd felt like she'd absorbed him into her orbit and animated him back to life. He'd been head over heels for her, but everything had come crashing down when he'd found out she'd been sleeping with the other rock star the entire time they'd been together.

Once again, his heart had been shattered. And then when he found Brit after her overdose, his heart had died right there in his chest.

It was in that moment that Logan knew all of it was his fault. The car crash. The overdose. The magical connection he'd shared with both women had ultimately killed them.

Logan promised himself that he'd would never, ever let it happen again.

And that was why he could not get involved with Georgia Exler. Between what he'd come to think of as his curse, and her magic where her written scenes were coming true, the only thing any relationship with her promised was tragedy.

Even as he promised himself he'd stay away from Georgia, he glanced up the stairs, longing to go up to her, to apologize, to take her into his arms and make her his, not just for the evening, but for forever.

An image of Georgia lying unconscious on her bedroom floor flashed in his mind.

He shot to his feet, his chest tight with alarm, and then ran up the stairs and busted into her bedroom. Logan froze when he spotted Georgia next to her bed, wearing a deep red slip nighty and balancing on one foot while holding herself steady with the walking stick.

"Logan? What the hell is wrong?" Georgia asked, clearly alarmed at the intrusion.

He let out a long breath as the pain in his chest started to ease. She was upright. Not lying on the floor passed out or dead from a brain aneurysm.

He wasn't exactly sure why he'd thought something had happened to her. He wasn't the one who had visions. Still, the sight of her standing there in her red negligee filled all those cold empty spaces in his heart. She was perfectly fine, just like she'd said she would be.

"Thank the gods," he muttered to himself and then let his gaze roam over her curvy frame.

"Logan!" she called out. "What are you doing up here?"

"Oh." He swallowed and met her gaze. "I was worried about you. I thought—"

She held up a hand. "You thought I'd lose my balance, fall on my face, and die of a traumatic brain injury?"

"Um, something like that," he admitted.

Georgia gritted her teeth. "Good night, Logan."

"Right." He nodded once and hurried back down the stairs, where he spent the entire night listening for any movement above, ready to help with even the smallest request.

Only none ever came, and by the time Logan finally got to sleep, the sun was already starting to light up the Northern California sky.

CHAPTER 11

*G*eorgia barely slept. How could she when Logan was downstairs? She was both relieved and humiliated that he'd stopped them the night before. She'd rationalized that she hadn't written a love scene, so anything they did beyond the kiss would be of his own free will.

Then he'd run as if he'd never really wanted to be with her at all.

His actions had nearly crushed her. Because when she'd been singing, pure magic had washed over her and she'd wanted nothing more than to be in his arms. It had been intoxicating, and she'd felt a pull she hadn't ever felt with anyone. Not even Nick.

That's why in the end, even though she'd wanted Logan desperately, whatever magic had washed over her had been terrifying. Terrifying enough that she'd been relieved when he'd disappeared downstairs.

Her feelings were all over the place, and the thought of facing him that morning made her want to bury her head under the covers and never come out again.

Unfortunately, she knew Logan would never let that happen, and she'd be damned if she let him find her wallowing with bedhead and morning breath. With a groan, she hauled herself out of bed, and using the walking stick, she hopped into the bathroom to make herself presentable. By the time she reemerged, she was physically exhausted but determined to make her way downstairs to the coffee maker.

Sweat coated Georgia's forehead as she worked her way toward the stairs. When she reached the top of the landing, she stared down the steps and nearly turned back. But then she'd have to ask Logan to carry her, and the idea of letting him manhandle her after he'd rejected her was out of the question. No way. She'd get down those stairs even if it meant crawling on all fours.

In the end, Georgia sat on the landing and went down on her butt one step at a time. It was slow going, but she made it unscathed and with her ankle intact.

"Georgia?" Logan said, his voice groggy from sleep.

She glanced over at him, still lying on the couch. His dark hair was tousled, and his chest was bare. Holy hell, he was sexy.

He sat up straight, causing the blanket to drop to his lap, exposing a six pack of abs she hadn't known existed. She swallowed hard and glanced away. "What are you doing?" he demanded. "I would've helped you down the stairs. Damn, you could've really hurt yourself."

"I needed coffee," she said, pleased that her voice wasn't hoarse with desire. "And I made it just fine. There's no need to worry." She used the banister to pull herself up until she was standing on her left leg. But when she glanced around, she realized she'd left the walking stick at the top of the stairs. "Son of a biscuit," she muttered and pushed her curls out of her eyes.

Logan darted off the couch and ran to her side. "What is it?"

His flannel sleep pants hung low on his hips, and there was an appealing happy trail that, under different circumstances, she'd be more than happy to trace with her fingertips... or tongue. Her face flushed with heat at the image running through her mind.

He slipped his arm around her waist and held out his other arm for her to use as support.

The minute she touched him, that sheen of magic washed over her again, and all she wanted to do was lean into him, touch him, taste him.

She cleared her throat. "It's nothing. I accidentally left the walking stick at the top of the stairs, so now I don't have anything that can help me get to the kitchen."

"I've got you." He scooped her up, doing the very thing she hoped to avoid by getting herself down the stairs.

She couldn't help herself when she pressed her head to his shoulder as he carried her into the kitchen. Being in his arms just felt *right*. But she knew once the moment was over she'd regret it. Regret losing that connection. Regret that she was too weak to tell him no. Regret that she liked being in his arms too much.

"Here." Logan set her down into one of the chairs at her kitchen table and pulled another one over so she could prop her ankle up. "I'll handle breakfast and the coffee. Just sit tight."

"If I had that walking stick, I could help," she said, watching as he moved around her kitchen effortlessly as if he'd been waking up in her house for months.

He glanced up from the coffee maker and raised one eyebrow. "You seem skeptical of my breakfast making skills."

She smirked and shook her head. "It's not that. I'm just not used to anyone waiting on me hand and foot." Georgia had always been fiercely independent, and even when Nick had been alive, it was rare that he'd cook for her. She glanced at the refrigerator, wondering when she'd last gone to the grocery store. More than a week ago, probably. "I am wondering what you're planning on feeding me since I probably don't have anything other than Pop-Tarts."

"Coffee first, then I'll see what I can whip up," he said easily.

It wasn't long before he set a cup of steaming Columbian roast in front of her. "Need anything? Creamer? Sweetener?"

"Creamer," she said, knowing she at least had that. Coffee was nonnegotiable in her house.

"On it." He retrieved the creamer, handed it to her, and then whistled as he rummaged through her fridge for something edible.

Georgia watched in fascination as he pulled out tortillas, a potato, cheese, and eggs.

Georgia had no idea she still had eggs in her fridge, and she was surprised the potato hadn't started to sprout roots.

"Got any salsa?" Logan asked her.

She shrugged. "Check the pantry. There might be something in there."

He nodded, and a few seconds later he pulled out a jar of salsa verde she didn't remember purchasing.

"I hope you're checking the expiration dates," she said with a chuckle. "You should know how it is when writers get into writer mode. Chips and cheese are a staple around here when I'm on deadline."

He laughed. "Don't worry, I checked. And there's no mold on the cheese." He winked at her and got to work on peeling the potato.

Georgia sat back in the chair, sipping her coffee as she stared out the back windows at the redwoods. The events from the day before kept running through her mind. Despite Logan's rejection of her the night before, he'd been nothing but kind and generous. She felt fairly ridiculous for being so upset at him the night before just because he hadn't wanted to fall into bed with her, especially since he was in her kitchen making her breakfast.

How long had it been since she'd experienced a morning like this one? Years. Not since college, she guessed, when she'd been dating the guy who was in culinary school. Why had she broken up with him? He'd made the best croissants she'd ever tasted outside of that one time she'd visited Paris. Oh, yeah. Because she'd met Nick, and the spark between them had been undeniable.

"More coffee?" Logan asked, standing near her with the pot in his hand.

She jerked and glanced up at him, startled by his presence. Eyeing her empty mug, she nodded. "Yes, please."

"Breakfast will be done in a few minutes. I just popped it into the oven to melt the cheese."

Georgia had been so busy thinking about the past twenty-four hours that she hadn't even paid attention to what he'd made. "Breakfast burritos?" she guessed, based on the ingredients.

"Breakfast enchiladas. They're a little basic, but they'll do."

"Basic? And here I was, ready to be satisfied with a Pop-Tart," Georgia said with a chuckle.

"Not on my watch." He winked.

A few minutes later, Logan was seated across from her with their breakfast plates in front of them. He raised his mug of coffee. "Here's to a new day."

"And new friendships," she added as she clinked her mug to his.

His lips curved into a pleased smile. "To new friendships."

Georgia knew she was lucky that Logan had come into her life, and even if a fling was out, she was going to do everything in her power to let him know how much she appreciated him. After she sipped her coffee, she dug into the enchilada. "Oh my gods," she said, her eyes rolling back in her head. "This is delicious."

Logan grinned at her. "And here you thought you only had Pop-Tarts."

"Hey!" she countered. "There's nothing wrong with Pop-Tarts. In my world, they're an entire food group."

He held his hands up in a surrender motion as his grin widened. "No offense intended."

She nodded. "But seriously, what did you put in these enchiladas?"

"Secret family recipe."

"Seriously? You're not going to tell me?"

Logan shook his head.

"That's it then. You're going to have to come over and make this for me every morning. I hope you like getting up at the crack of dawn."

"Everyday?" he asked with a raised eyebrow. "No time off for good behavior?"

"Okay, fine," she said with an exaggerated sigh. "You can have one day off per week. Sundays can be Pop-Tart day."

His eyes glinted with humor. "Brown Sugar Cinnamon?"

"Is there any other kind?"

"Georgia," Logan said, "I think this is going to be a beautiful friendship."

CHAPTER 12

Georgia moved across the sidewalk like a champ with her new crutches. Logan had taken her to Eureka to pick them up, and then after she insisted she could drive with her left foot, he'd driven her back to Keating Hollow and left her and her car at Charming Herbals after his brother met them there.

She waited until they drove off before she crutched her way over to the front door. Before she could push her way in, Bree Burgess, the owner of the shop, was already there holding the glass door open for her.

"Thank you," Georgia said, grateful for the help. "I've taken to these pretty quickly, but navigating doors is still a challenge."

"Of course," Bree said. The shop owner led Georgia over to a tufted couch and gestured for her to take a seat. "Please sit. I'll grab everything you need."

Georgia's first instinct was to decline, but she was exhausted after not sleeping much the night before and gratefully sank down onto the couch. She smiled up at the pretty brunette. Her curls were piled up into a bun, and her smile reached her kind green eyes. "Thank you. It's been a challenging couple of days."

Bree eyed Georgia's wrapped ankle. "What happened?"

Georgia let out a bark of laughter. "Oh, that's a story, and the reason I'm here."

"I have time." Bree perched beside Georgia and turned to her with an expectant look on her face. "Let's hear it."

Georgia glanced at her ankle, tried to move it slightly, and winced. Okay, she guessed she was starting there. "Okay, first things first. Yesterday I suffered a hairline fracture. Levi Kelley worked his magic and said it'd be all better in a couple of weeks, but I could really use something to help with the dull ache."

"I've got just the thing." Bree jumped up and went straight to one of her glass cabinets. A moment later, she was back with a potion bottle. "Take a tablespoon of this once in the morning and once at night. Should numb the pain and help with the healing."

The light blue glass bottle was frosted and felt cool in Georgia's hand. "Thank you. I appreciate this."

"Absolutely. That's what I'm here for." She gave Georgia a kind smile. "What else can I do for you?"

"You remember that story I was going to tell you?" Georgia asked.

"Yes," Bree said with a nod. "I'm ready."

Georgia blew out a breath. "You know I'm a writer?"

"Sure. Who doesn't?"

Keating Hollow was a small town. Keeping a low profile would be nearly impossible. Not that Georgia cared. It was nice that most of the residents of the town supported her by buying her signed books at Hollow Books. "So, I started a new book, and right after I wrote the first scene, I met Logan Malone, and the events of our meeting were remarkably similar to the scene I'd just written."

"Really?" Bree's eyes lit up with interest. "How similar?"

"I wrote that the heroine sat on a piece of cake, and then what did I do?"

"You sat on a piece of cake?" Bree guessed.

"Bingo. That was disconcerting, but I brushed it off until it happened with two more scenes. Or more accurately, a scene and part of an outline." Georgia bit her bottom lip and waited for the herbalist to process what she'd said.

"So... You're saying that you write a scene and then it happens in real life?"

Georgia nodded. "I know it sounds crazy, but I wrote a scene where the heroine falls while hiking and the hero carries her off to safety. In the next one, the hero and heroine are messing around with the guitar, and they share their first kiss." Georgia's cheeks warmed, making her certain that she was blushing. "After that, I've been afraid to write anything else for fear I'll manifest it into existence."

Bree tapped her finger against her chin. "So three incidents. Did they all happen with the same man?"

"Yes. With Logan." Georgia leaned back into the couch with her arms crossed over her chest.

"Interesting." Bree stood, nodding to herself. "Very, very interesting."

"What's so interesting about it?" Georgia asked, because as far as she was concerned, it wasn't so much interesting as it was horrifying. "I need to figure out how to stop it."

Bree turned around to study her. "You don't like Logan?"

Georgia had the desire to let out a laugh, though she knew it would be hollow. That was the biggest problem; she liked

Logan far too much. "It's not that. I just feel like I might be coercing him into something he doesn't want to do. Is that possible?"

"It is possible." The herbalist moved back to the couch and once again perched next to Georgia. "What kind of witch are you?"

Georgia shrugged. "No idea. I've never had any real powers before this."

"Really?" Her eyes widened. "That *is* interesting. Any family history of spirit witches?"

"According to my aunt, I have a great-aunt who had visions."

"That makes a lot of sense." Bree shifted back onto the couch and pulled one leg up, getting comfortable. "I'd guess that you are a spirit witch and you're getting visions while writing."

"They don't feel like visions," Georgia insisted. "I just make up the scenes in my head."

"Maybe you just think you're making them up," she said with a shrug of her shoulder. "While it's possible to use magic to compel people to behave a certain way, I highly doubt it's happening just from you writing it down."

"But how do we know for sure?" Georgia asked. "How do I know that if I write a fight scene or something tragic happens to one of my characters, that it won't happen in real life?"

"There's no way to know for sure," the pretty brunette said. She averted her green eyes, but not before Georgia noticed that they held unshed tears.

"Bree?" Georgia asked. "Are you all right?"

She nodded and then let out a choked laugh as she dabbed at one eye. "Sorry. I... um, this hits a little close to home."

Georgia placed a gentle hand on her arm. "I'm sorry. I didn't mean to upset you."

"No need to apologize," she said, shaking her head. "I'm the one who's sorry. I didn't mean to break down on you like that. It's just that…" She sucked in a breath. "Grief has a way of sneaking up on you sometimes, doesn't it?"

"It does," Georgia said quietly, thinking about all the times she'd broken down doing mundane things like baking cupcakes or planting sunflowers. They were always things that brought back memories of her own mother. The pain would come out of nowhere, reminding her that she'd never see her mother's smile or hear her infectious laugh again. Those moments left her feeling unable to breathe with chest pains that were caused by a broken heart rather than some sort of medical condition. "If there's anything I can do, I'm here."

"Thanks, but I'm okay." Bree sat up straighter. Her eyes were clear of tears, but the sadness still remained. "My mom was a seer. The visions came to her in poetry that she wrote."

Georgia let out a gasp. "Really?"

Bree nodded. "Only it sounds a bit different because all of her poems came true. She only ever wrote when a vision took over."

"Were they… um, what kinds of things did she write about?" Georgia asked, terrified of what Bree might reveal.

"All kinds of things. Love, friendship, heartbreak… and in the end, death." Bree reached out for Georgia's hand. "She knew her time was ending."

Georgia let out a gasp. "I'm so sorry. That must have been really upsetting for all of you."

Bree nodded. "It was at first, but then because we knew the end was near, we turned her last days into a celebration of life.

You know, bucket list type of things, and those are some of my most cherished memories."

"Wow. That's not what I was expecting you to say. How wonderful for you both."

"For all of us, really." Bree brushed a stray lock of hair out of her eyes. "My sisters were able to come for a visit, and the three of us were all together for the first time in years. My mom loved it. So even though some of her visions were a stress for her, in the end they really ended up being a blessing. We'd never have had that time together if not for her gift."

Georgia mulled that over, wondering if the scenes coming true in her book were actually a blessing in disguise. If only she knew they were actual visions of the future instead of something she was making happen just by writing it out. She sighed. "I understand what you're trying to tell me, but what if I don't want this gift? Is there a way to stop it?"

Bree pursed her lips as she considered Georgia's question. "I suppose you could try an herbal suppressant. It would work to dull your magic, but it might have side effects, like altering your mood, energy level, or motivation."

"You mean it could make me depressed?" Georgia asked, wrinkling her nose.

"Not necessarily depression, but anything you take that will dull magic can be problematic in other areas."

Nothing about that sounded appealing to Georgia.

"Has anything awful happened?" Bree asked.

Georgia raised one eyebrow. "It depends on what you call awful. I've sat on a piece of cake, got roped into karaoke, suffered a hairline fracture, and practically threw myself at someone who clearly wasn't interested. If one could die of embarrassment, they'd be planning my funeral as we speak."

Bree chuckled. "None of that sounds catastrophic."

"No, it doesn't. I just… It's unnerving, you know?"

"Yes, I do." Bree gave her a sympathetic smile. "If I were you, I'd just write the book of my heart. Stay true to your story and have fun with it. If I've learned anything from my mom's experience, it's that you can't really control fate."

"What if I'm manifesting things to happen?" Georgia asked, unable to let that go.

"So what if you are? People manifest things all the time. Free will still exists. Just because you write something, that doesn't mean you've taken away someone's choice."

Georgia nodded, but she wasn't convinced and still felt apprehensive.

"Listen, I can give you some of the herbal suppressant, and if you feel like you need it, it'll be there. If not, no harm done."

"Yeah, okay." Georgia nodded, feeling better to have something in her arsenal if she needed it.

CHAPTER 13

*L*ogan let out a frustrated growl as he hit the delete button, erasing all the notes he'd made for his next book. He'd jotted down a dozen ideas, but not one of them grabbed him. He was starting to feel as if his creative well was completely empty, and it frustrated the hell out of him.

"How's it going?" Seth asked as he walked into the kitchen.

"It's not." Logan slammed the laptop closed and sat back in his chair at the breakfast table.

Seth raised both eyebrows. "Writer's block?"

"Something like that." He stood and walked into the kitchen to grab another cup of coffee.

"Maybe it'll help if we talk about it." Seth helped himself to a piece of coffee cake from the white box on the counter and took a large bite, causing the crumbs to scatter over the tile floor.

"Jeez, Seth. Could you use a plate next time?" Logan stared down at the floor pointedly.

"Sorry," he said through a mouthful of cake.

"No you aren't." Logan grabbed the broom from a closet and nudged his brother out of the way.

Seth eyed him. "You really are having trouble writing, aren't you? I'm not sure I've ever seen you willingly do housework."

"Shut up," Logan said with a chuckle. "Who do you think cleans this place, Snow White's menagerie?"

"I'm sure if you could figure out how to spell the critters outside to mop your floors, you would."

"Okay, this conversation is getting weird." Logan finished cleaning up his brother's mess and then returned the broom to the closet.

"So," Seth said. "Are you going to answer my question?"

"Which one is that?"

"The one where I asked if you want to talk about what's bothering you." Seth leaned against the counter and crossed one ankle over the other.

"Technically, you didn't actually ask me a question. You made a statement, and I ignored it." Logan took a sip of his coffee and stared his brother down.

Seth rolled his eyes. "Whatever, dude. You know it will help to talk it out."

"You want to talk plot points for my next book? Have thoughts on the hero's journey?" Logan knew what, or more precisely who, Seth wanted to talk about, but Logan would rather have his liver harvested than tell his brother what happened the night before at Georgia's. Now that he was home, all he wanted to do was run back to her house and pick up where they'd left off. Or at least that's what his body wanted him to do. His head was still telling him to stay the hell away.

"Not on your life." Seth's lips twitched. "But if you want to work on the bridge of a song I'm messing around with, we could do that."

"Sure." Anything to get away from the subject of Georgia.

His eyes widened. "You really *do* have it bad if you're willing to work on a song instead of talking about the woman you spent the night with last night."

"We didn't spend the night together," Logan insisted. "She slept in her room, and I slept on the couch."

"Judging by those bags under your eyes, you didn't do much sleeping at all, brother."

"You're not going to let this go, are you?" Logan asked, narrowing his eyes.

"Nope." Seth brushed a lock of his dark blond hair out of his eyes and smirked. "What kept you up all night?"

Logan hung his head and let out a sigh. After a moment, he looked up and said, "I can't risk it again."

"Risk what? Being in love? You deserve to be happy, Logan," Seth said, his voice low and full of sympathy.

He snorted out a humorless laugh. "Love. Are you serious right now? You know what I'm talking about. First Cherry, then Brit. If anything happened to Georgia, that would be the end of me. I'd never forgive myself. How am I supposed to have a relationship when I know that I'm the reason..." He shook his head, unable to finish the sentence.

"How many times do I have to tell you that you aren't cursed?" Seth demanded. All his understanding had fled, and anger flashed in his eyes. "Bad things happen sometimes."

"Yeah!" Logan shot back. "Bad shit happens. But not like that."

"Like what?" Seth moved to stand toe-to-toe with his brother. "What makes your experience so different than anyone else who loses someone they love? All you ever say is it was your fault. How?"

"I don't want to talk about this." Logan pushed away from the counter and started to move through his house.

"Of course you don't. You never do. If you don't talk about it, then you never have to think about opening up your heart again."

Logan whirled around and stalked back to his brother. "You have no idea what you're talking about."

"Oh, I don't?" Seth spat. "You don't think I remember how you were lost for so long after Cherry's accident or how you completely shut down after Brit's overdose? I was there, Logan. I was the one who saw you through the worst of it. I know you blamed it all on yourself, that you still wear that guilt like a punishment. I need you to hear this." He took a small step closer, and all the anger drained from his voice when he said, "You deserve to live, to be happy. And I deserve to have my brother back."

Logan blinked. "What do you mean, you deserve to have your brother back? I'm here. I've always been here for you."

Seth ran a frustrated hand through his tousled hair. "You're right, you have. But you're... not the same. More of a shell of who you used to be. You shut down, and I haven't seen that spark of life light you up from the inside in years." He paused for a second. "Well, not until this week anyway when you talk about Georgia. She lights you up, brother. It'd be a damned shame if you threw that all away because you think you're the reason we lost Cherry."

"And Brit," Logan added under his breath.

"Brit's responsible for what happened to Brit, and we both know it," Seth said. "I know you loved her, and in her own way she loved you, too. But she had problems, Logan. Ones that were beyond your help. It's not your fault."

Intellectually, Logan knew his brother was right, but it didn't change the fact that he'd felt like their intense love affair was what caused Brit's ultimate downfall. It was different with Cherry, but he also knew she'd have never been in the car that night if she hadn't been desperate to be there for him. There was nothing she wouldn't have done for Logan. He blew out a long breath. "That spark I had with Cherry, and to a certain extent Brit, too… It's there with Georgia. And it scares the hell out of me."

Sympathy swam in Seth's blue gaze. "I hear you. I really do. But do you really want to spend the rest of your time on this earth going through the motions, buried behind your computer, or do you want to live?"

He knew his answer. More than anything, he wanted to live, to love intensely. To spend his days and nights with the gorgeous paranormal writer who completely fascinated him. But his guilt just wouldn't let him.

Seth let out a tired sigh. "Just do me a favor, will you?"

"What's that?"

"Consider the possibility that you are not to blame for past events, and that both Cherry and Brit made their own choices. And while what happened to both of them was tragic, it wasn't a curse. It was just life. Sometimes it sucks. Hard. But you are *not* cursed."

Logan opened his mouth to speak, but Seth put his hand up, stopping him.

"No need to answer or argue. Just think about what I've said. Okay?"

"Okay," Logan said in a hoarse voice. "I'll try."

"Good." Seth shoved his hands into his pockets and rocked

back on his heels. "Well, now that we're done with that conversation, I'm not sure where we go from here."

"You could tell me what happened between you and Cal," Logan said.

"Next." Seth stared him down, indicating they weren't going to talk about that subject.

"I see. We can have a full-on therapy session about my issues, but you won't even tell me the catalyst for your boyfriend walking out on you and messing with the band. Is that how this is going to be?"

"Shit." Seth stared out the window. "He thinks I cheated on him."

"Did you?" Logan asked, unable to hide the judgment that colored his tone.

Seth gave him an evil glare. "Are you serious right now?"

Logan shrugged one shoulder. "You know I don't trust my judgment. If someone asked me, I'd say hell no, you'd never do that. But what do I know? It's not like we spend much time together these days."

"That time's about to get shorter if you don't take your head out of your ass," Seth shot back. "No, I didn't cheat on him. But you know how it is being in a band. People say all kinds of shit to try to pump themselves up. One of the roadies was spreading rumors that I was slipping into restrooms with him every chance I got. And that gossip, combined with his jealousy over the success of "The One," made Cal just lose it."

"The One" was the band's hit single that Seth had written about his ex. Cal had originally done the vocals for the record, but before they could release it, a version Seth had done and put on his YouTube channel before the band had been signed went viral. The label made them re-record it with Seth on lead vocals, and Cal had been bitter ever since. "You do know you deserve better than that, right?"

"You mean I deserve someone who trusts me? Yeah, I know."

"And someone who doesn't try to suck all the joy out of your success. He should be happy for you. That song is incredible, and you sound incredible singing it. If he can't see far enough past his own ego to be happy for you, then you're better off without him."

Seth pressed his lips together into a thin line as his jaw worked.

Logan knew he'd hit a nerve. "I only want the best for you, little brother. You know that, right?"

"Right back at you, big brother."

They were silent as they each looked anywhere but at each other.

Finally, Logan chuckled at their awkwardness and jerked his head toward the door. "Come on. Let's go do something fun."

"Fun? I didn't realize my big brother knew what fun was," Seth said in a shocked tone. "Does it involve weeding the yard? Getting the oil changed in your car? Heading to the dry cleaners?"

"Dry cleaners? Who do you think I am?" Logan asked.

"A stuffy writer type? I dunno. Since when do you do anything fun?"

Logan rolled his eyes. "Shut it." He downed the rest of his coffee then jerked his head toward the door. "Let's go."

CHAPTER 14

Georgia stood in her office, leaning on one of her crutches as she stared at her empty plot board. Usually by the time she made it this far into her manuscript, she had all the scenes worked out and was ready for her fingers to fly. The ideas were there in her mind, but she just couldn't bring herself to write anything down.

She desperately wanted to believe that Bree was on to something. That she couldn't really control what happened. That everyone had free will and whatever Georgia decided to write, it was either fate or just a vision.

The problem was that Georgia often wrote traumatic or very painful issues for her characters to work through. If she wrote that now, she'd never forgive herself for potentially bringing pain to someone. She clutched the blue marker and took a deep breath. She couldn't just not write. How would she pay her bills if she just stopped? Georgia had been a writer for the better part of a decade. Changing careers, while possible, would break her.

That meant if she was going to put this book out, she had to make it fun. No tragedies. Just a werewolf falling in love with a sweet witch who helped him heal from his past trauma. No need to go through new pain, right? Working through old pain was plenty.

With her lips curved into a small smile, Georgia got busy scribbling on her board.

When she had the next fifteen chapters mapped out, she pumped her fist into the air and decided it was time for a coffee break. When she returned to work again, her heroine was going to take the hero ice-skating for the first time. And if they were lucky, they'd melt the ice with their connection.

An hour later, Georgia crutched her way into Incantation Café with her laptop bag on one shoulder. The place was mostly empty, and she opted for the table in the front window instead of the one in the back. It was a gloriously sunny fall day, and she wanted to feel the sun on her face as she put words on the page.

"Georgia!" Hanna called as she hurried over to her friend. "I heard about your ankle. Are you okay?"

"I'm all right, thanks to Levi." She nodded down at her ankle. "I made a stop at the healers' office before coming in. Gerry says Levi did an excellent job and it's healing nicely. I still can't put weight on it for a while, and she gave me a prescription for a pain potion if I need it, but so far I'm managing."

"Good. That's really good." Hanna pulled out a chair for her. "Sit. I'll get your latte and a pumpkin cupcake. We put a cream cheese filling in them, and oh my goddess, you are going to die when you taste it."

"Sounds amazing. Thank you. But make the latte a mocha with extra whip. I'm feeling... decadent today."

"Extra whip. You're my kind of girl." Hanna winked and hurried back to the counter.

Georgia opened her laptop, intending to start typing, but she was distracted when the invisible bells on the door chimed. The man who walked in had a familiarity to him that she couldn't quite put her finger on. He was tall and broad shouldered with wavy dark blond hair. She didn't recognize him, but his gait and the way he moved made her think that she'd met him before. She couldn't keep her eyes off him as he moved to the counter.

As soon as he ordered and Georgia heard his voice, she knew.

Seth. Logan's brother. There was no question. They had the same gravelly voice. The kind that was just made for singing. Not to mention that while their coloring was different, they had the same facial features. There was no doubt they were related.

"That one must be for Logan," Hanna said with a laugh. "He's the only person I know who orders nonfat caramel vanilla lattes with four shots of espresso and extra whip. I mean, it's kind of like ordering three desserts and a Diet Coke."

Seth laughed. "I told him something similar just a few minutes ago, but he swears it's just because he likes the taste of nonfat better." He shrugged. "If it makes him happy, I'm happy."

"That's my motto." Hanna got busy fulfilling orders.

Georgia sat back, watching Seth in fascination. He was handsome, but in a rugged way, while Logan was more polished. She supposed that could be a function of their life choices considering Logan was a writer and Seth was in a band.

"Hey," Seth said with a nod when he spotted her watching him.

Georgia felt herself flush all over. "Sorry. I didn't mean to stare. It's just that you remind me so much of Logan. I find it fascinating."

He eyed her with interest. "You know my brother?"

She nodded. "Yes. He's been a good friend. Not everyone is willing and able to carry a grown woman out of the woods when she messes up her ankle."

Recognition lit in his eyes. "Ah, you must be Georgia." He walked over and held his hand out to her. "I'm Seth."

She shook his hand. "It's nice to meet you. Are you in town long?"

He shrugged one shoulder. "We'll see. It depends on what happens with my band." He gestured to an empty chair at her table. "Mind if I sit while I wait for my order?"

"Not at all. Especially if you'll tell me all your brother's secrets," she teased. His expression turned guarded, and Georgia immediately understood she'd said something wrong. "I'm sorry. I was just joking. I didn't mean anything by that."

He blew out a breath and sat back in his chair. "No worries. I'm sure I overreacted. It's just that we've both had our share of intrusive press. Show business is really invasive, you know?"

"Not really, but I can imagine." She let out a soft chuckle. "Unless a writer is a household name, no one seems to really care what we get up to. I'm surprised the media has hounded Logan. Was it bad?"

"It was a long time ago, before he switched gears to be a writer. I heard he played his guitar for you one night, so you know he's a musician. But did you know he was in a band?"

"He mentioned something about it. Said he was better with words."

Seth shook his head slowly.

Georgia raised an eyebrow. "You don't think he's a great writer? It's hard to argue with his success."

"It's not that," Seth said with a slight chuckle. "No doubt he has his fans, but to say he's better at words? No. Not in this lifetime. You heard him play, right?"

"Sure. He's very good on the guitar," she agreed. Really, really good.

"His voice is even better. His band was on the verge of making it huge when he quit. They were set to go on a worldwide tour and had a hit song. But after the accident, he just gave it all up."

"What accident?" Georgia asked, leaning forward. "And what band?"

"His first band was called Jump Back. They had recorded a song for a kids' show that was semi popular. But it was his second band, the rock band Halo, that he put his heart and soul into. Look them up. I'm pretty sure there's still a Wikipedia page for them."

"I will." Georgia peered at him. "Something tells me Logan wouldn't necessarily want you talking about this. Why are you telling me?"

"Because, Georgia, my brother has been through a lot. More than most. And he could really use some fun in his life. It looks to me like you might be the one who could bring back that side of him. But it might take a little effort, and I wanted you to know why."

Hanna arrived at that moment with both of their orders. She placed Georgia's order in front of her and handed Seth a to-go tray and bag.

"Thanks, Hanna," Georgia said.

Seth stood after adding his own thanks. "I better get back to

Magical Notes before they come looking for me." He glanced at Georgia. "It was nice meeting you."

"You, too," she said, dying to ask him more questions about his brother, but she didn't want to put him on the spot in front of Hanna.

After he stepped outside, Hanna turned to her, her eyes sparkling with interest. "What were you two talking about?"

"Logan. Did you know he was in a band before he was a writer?" Georgia asked.

"Yeah. Pretty sure I knew he did some song for a kid's show. Why?"

"No reason. His brother said something about it." Georgia picked up her cupcake, took a bite, and let out a loud moan as the pumpkin spice and cream cheese filling sent sparks of delight over her tongue. "Oh my gods," she whispered reverently to Hanna. "This is incredible."

Hanna beamed. "Thanks. It took a little magic to get it right, but I couldn't be happier with the results."

"Magic?" Georgia asked.

Hanna just winked and then walked back to the counter.

"I'm going to need a half dozen of these to take home," she called after Hanna.

"I'm on it," the café owner called back.

Georgia opened her laptop and searched for a band named Halo while she finished the cupcake and sipped her mocha. After a few clicks, she had the Wikipedia page open for the band. There wasn't much there, just a write-up of the four members, a line about their one-hit wonder, and then a notation that one of their members died in a tragic car accident. The woman's name was Cherry Chance. She clicked the link to the citation and scanned the article.

"Oh, no," Georgia whispered when she realized that Cherry

had died while she was rushing to meet Logan at a private airfield on a stormy night because of a last-minute booking on a late-night talk show. It was a brutal accident, and the photo attached was heartbreaking. Logan was at the scene, his face full of anguish as he held her lifeless body.

An update to the article indicated that the band broke up two months later and that Logan wasn't seen or heard from until three years later when his then-girlfriend was found dead after committing suicide.

Georgia rubbed at the ache in her chest and had to wipe away the tears pooling in her eyes. Seth was right. Logan had suffered more than most, and he did deserve to have someone to help him have some fun.

It wasn't until Georgia was out the door with her bag of cupcakes and crutching her way to her car that she realized it had happened again. Her notes for her next chapter lined up perfectly with what she planned to do when it came to Logan. The hero had a tragic past, and the heroine was going to encourage him to move forward by helping him have some fun. Except Georgia vetoed the ice-skating idea. There was no way she was going to end up on the ice anytime soon.

But that didn't mean she couldn't find something better. She just had to get creative.

CHAPTER 15

"One more?" Logan asked while strumming the guitar.

Levi, who was on the drums, tapped out a quick beat. "Hell yeah. I don't have anywhere to be."

"How about an original?" Seth said, running his fingers over the keyboard.

"You have a new one you want to try?" Logan asked his brother. They'd been in the back room of Magical Notes for the past hour playing everything from Prince to Red Hot Chili Peppers. Logan knew his brother would love playing without the pressure of dealing with his band, and he'd been right. Seth had been giving it his all, pounding out notes on the piano while lending his voice for the vocals. And Logan had been content to play his heart out on the guitar.

"There's something I've kind of been working on. Do you mind?" Seth asked.

"Not at all," Levi chimed in. "Let's hear it."

Seth nodded and started to play. The opening was a soft bittersweet sound and was the type of opening that made one really stop and listen. Then after a pause, his fingers started to fly as the tempo turned dramatic. Seth nodded to the other two, indicating they should follow along.

Logan jumped in, picking up what Seth was laying down right away. It took Levi a few tries but he finally found the beat, and Logan knew that with some refining, the music Seth had created was going to be something special.

They jammed for what felt like forever until Seth changed the tempo back to the opening. Logan and Levi let their last notes fade away, giving Seth the spotlight. And when his fingers finally came to a stop, they were all silent, soaking in the fact that they all knew they'd been a part of something that would touch people's souls.

Seth cleared his throat. "Again? I started some lyrics."

Logan and Levi both nodded and waited for the music to start again.

"Red light, sun light. All I wanted that morning was to hold you till the night," Seth sang in a haunting voice.

Goosebumps popped up on Logan's skin, and he knew, just *knew*, this was Seth's breakthrough song.

"That was the day you told me you were mine, but then the call came. You said we were fine. You were mine. Red light, sun light, you were gone that night."

The fast drumbeat lit a fire in Logan's veins, and while Seth sang what had to be his epic breakup song, Logan felt every last note of it in his soul. It was bittersweet, full of loss, love, and jealousy. It would resonate, no doubt.

"You said you'd be back," Levi chimed in. *"That it was just for the contract. You were mine, we were fine. Midnight, moonlight, what happened to waking up together in the sunlight?"*

Seth nodded to Levi, and together they threw out lines, playing off each other. All the while, Logan played on, sure in his conviction that he was watching the start of something magical.

When the last notes faded away, Logan let out a low whistle.

"That was... wow," Levi said, his eyes wide.

"There's something there, right?" Seth asked.

"It's a goddammed hit, Seth." Logan walked over to Levi and gave him a clap on his shoulder. "I had no idea you could sing like that."

Levi shrugged, his face turning slightly pink. "I've really only practiced in my shower."

Seth laughed. "It's time to get out of the bathroom, son, because I'm gonna need you to help me lay down those vocals."

Levi's mouth dropped open. Then he swallowed and cleared his throat. "Are you serious?"

Seth glanced at Logan. "It had the magic, didn't it?"

Logan nodded. "Definitely. It'd be a crime if you didn't collaborate."

"It's settled then," Seth said, getting up from the piano and walking over to the drummer. "How about we put our heads together and work on refining our lyrics?"

"Uh, yeah, okay," Levi said. He jumped up, knocking over one of the cymbals. It fell with a loud crash. "Shit." He scrambled to put it back in place.

Seth chuckled and jerked his head. "Come on. Let's head over to the café so we can work."

Logan watched the pair of them disappear back into the front of the shop. Then as he was gathering his coat, he heard the light sound of someone entering the room. He turned around and spotted Georgia standing just inside the doorframe, leaning on her crutches.

She tilted her head to one side as she smiled at him. "That was impressive."

"I was just following their lead. The song is Seth's, and now Levi's, I guess." He grabbed his jacket and shrugged it on. "How long have you been out there?"

"Just a few minutes. I came to see if you have a few hours to hang out today."

Was that a nervous thread he detected in her voice? He wasn't sure. "I don't have anything on my calendar. What did you have in mind?"

Her smile widened. "Do you like wine?"

"Sure. Who doesn't?"

"Good. The Pelshes have a winery, and I've been meaning to get out there to check it out. You game?"

He nodded toward the door. "After you."

LOGAN OPENED the car door for Georgia and handed her the crutches.

"Thanks." She hopped out on one foot, wielding the crutches as if she'd been using them for weeks instead of just a few days. "This way."

He followed her up the sidewalk, taking in the beautiful surroundings. There were grapevines on three sides of the building, and they'd turned gorgeous shades of orange and yellow.

"It's harvest season," Georgia said. "If we're lucky, we might get to see their process."

Logan had to admit that'd be cool. But he honestly didn't care what they did. He was just enjoying spending time with her. On the drive to the vineyard, they'd chatted about their favorite authors, movies, and even music. She'd raved about Seth, and even knew a couple of his band's songs.

He'd been so relaxed that when he'd talked about how he and Seth had gotten into music, he'd slipped and mentioned something about his own band. He'd been surprised when Georgia hadn't asked him any questions about Halo, but then quickly realized that she must already know and was leaving the subject alone on purpose. He'd wanted to kiss her for it, but considering they were supposed to be just friends, he'd refrained.

They reached the sliding barn door, and Logan opened it for her.

"Thanks," she said softly as she moved past him into the building.

Logan followed her and was surprised to see they were the only ones there. "Are they open?"

"Yep." She made her way to the bar and took a seat on the stool. After a moment, a menu appeared out of thin air and floated down to the bar in front of her. "Are you hungry?"

"A little bit." He sat next to her and glanced over her shoulder even as his own menu appeared. "What are you in the mood for?"

She turned her head and their eyes caught. The air was suddenly heavy between them. Logan couldn't help it when his gaze landed on her lips. *Holy hell*, he thought. His attraction to her was off the charts.

Georgia leaned back and took a breath. "I'm thinking the seared tuna or the savory crepes."

"Both. And the goat cheese ravioli."

"Sounds perfect." Georgia placed both menus together and then let out a tiny gasp as two wine glasses appeared in front of them.

"Did you know this place was charmed like this?" Logan asked her.

"No. Not at all. Hanna told me they were doing some new and interesting things here, but I thought she was referring to the cider business, not turning the tasting room into a magical oasis. Though I shouldn't be surprised since Hanna told me her mother's a very talented air witch"

"It's a work in progress," an older woman who had the same eyes as Hanna said as she walked in. "Hi, I'm Mary. Welcome to the Pelsh Winery."

"Hi, Mary. The menu looks amazing," Logan said.

"Thank you. It is. But wait until you taste the wine. That's the real show." Mary got to work setting up a flight of wine for them, and before he knew it, the food they'd talked about but never actually ordered arrived.

By the time the wine glasses and plates were empty, Logan was relaxed and having a fantastic time with Georgia. She was easy to talk to and fun to laugh with.

"Have you ever just been so preoccupied with a plotline that you weren't really aware of your surroundings?" she asked Logan.

"Um, I guess. Like when someone is trying to talk to you, but you don't hear them because you're so caught up?"

"Sure. But I'm even worse than that. One time before I moved here, I was staying at a vacation rental while trying to meet a deadline. I was outside, pacing around while I worked through a plot problem. I was so out of it that I ended up walking right into the pool." She chuckled. "The funniest part of that story is that when I came up sputtering, I suddenly figured out the solution."

"That was lucky," he said, grinning at her. He loved a woman who could laugh at herself.

"I thought so. Wanna know what I did the next time I was having trouble?" Her eyes twinkled with mischief.

"You tried the shower?" he asked, knowing a lot of writers did their best thinking while standing under a stream of water where they couldn't be distracted.

"Nope. I found the nearest pool and threw myself in."

He shook his head. "Did it work?"

"Not even remotely. However, I entertained the neighbors. It was their pool."

Logan threw his head back and laughed. "Jeez, Georgia. You're something else."

"I try."

Mary appeared again, her eyes twinkling with excitement. "Are you ready for the tour?"

"There's a tour?" Georgia asked and then looked down at her foot. "How far is it? I can crutch around for a bit, but if we're talking a significant walk, I might need to pass on this one."

"Don't worry. There's no walking necessary." Mary gestured for them to follow her.

Logan held out an arm for Georgia so she could steady herself as she slid off the stool and got her crutches in place, and then he followed her out the back door where there was a horseless hay wagon waiting.

"Your chariot awaits," Mary said. "Climb in and enjoy the afternoon exploring the grounds."

"I'm game if you are," Georgia said.

Logan nodded. He couldn't think of anywhere he'd rather be.

CHAPTER 16

"This is more than I bargained for," Georgia said, laughing as the wagon bumped along the dirt path through the winery.

"Really?" Logan asked, his face so full of joy it nearly made Georgia cry.

She clutched the edge of the wooden seat as her backside bounced up and down on the hard surface. "Let's just say I would've brought a pillow for my tushie if I'd known it was going to be this rough of a ride."

"Ah, poor thing. But at least Mary supplied a pillow for your foot."

Georgia had to admit that Mary Pelsh really was a keeper. She hadn't let the wagon leave the barn until she was certain Georgia's ankle was safe from further damage. "The Pelsh Winery is so getting a five-star review on Yelp."

"High praise."

"Do I know how to pick em or what?" Georgia asked him.

"You certainly do," he said, suddenly sounding serious as he slipped his hand over hers and squeezed her fingers.

Georgia's heart picked up a beat. When she'd decided to take Logan out for the afternoon, she'd never expected it to be anything more than friendship. She wasn't naive. The chemistry between them was off the charts, but after he'd pulled away, she assumed they just weren't going to cross that line.

You did write about this, a voice in the back of her mind reminded her.

So what if she'd written something similar? That scene in particular only brought joy. If she was making this happen, then so be it. Everyone deserved happiness. Georgia quickly pushed the thought aside and threaded her fingers through Logan's. When he tightened his grip around hers, her insides went gooey. There wasn't much that she loved more than feeling a connection to someone. And it had been far too long since she'd felt anything but lonely.

"What's that?" Logan asked as he squinted ahead of them.

Georgia followed his gaze and frowned. "Some sort of pond?"

As they got closer, Georgia squinted and then let out a bark of laughter when she recognized where they were headed. "I can't believe this."

"Can't believe what? It looks like an ice-skating rink." He pointed toward a small building and some benches that were lined up at one end. "They even have a shack for ice skates." He glanced down at her foot. "Oh, right. Maybe next time?"

"There's going to be a next time?" Georgia asked before she could stop herself.

He glanced down at their clasped hands. "I think that's likely, don't you?"

"Yes. I just didn't want to presume anything."

He chuckled and lifted her hand to his lips.

The kiss he gave her sent shivers over her skin, causing an involuntary sigh that made her sound like a lovesick teenager.

His lips twitched into a tiny half smile, indicating he'd noticed, but he didn't say anything as he clasped both of his hands over the one of hers that he held in his lap.

"I think you should do some ice-skating, and I'll video you for our highlights reel," Georgia teased.

"Not on your life," he said, shaking his head. "The moment I step out there, I'll end up breaking my tailbone."

"Seriously? Have you never been ice-skating before?" she asked.

"Nope."

"But you probably were a skateboarder, right?"

He eyed her. "How did you know that?"

"Just a lucky guess," she said. He had the lanky but muscular build of a man who was athletic but didn't spend a lot of time in the gym. "When do I get to see your moves?"

"Right about the time you show me yours when you're plotting near the pool."

Georgia chuckled. "Yeah, okay. One of these days I'm going to invite you out and take you up on that."

"Sure you are."

The wagon jerked to a stop right next to the shack near the ice-skating rink.

"Oh, no, wagon," Georgia said. "We're not getting out."

The wagon didn't move.

She glanced around, looking for a button or a lever that would put the wagon back in gear. But there wasn't anything. Not even a blanket in case they got cold. "Well, this is going to be awkward when we die of exposure out here."

"Dramatic much?" Logan asked.

"Not if we're left out here all night. You have no idea how cold I get at night."

"I'll keep you warm," he promised even as he started to climb out of the wagon.

Georgia was still daydreaming about how exactly he'd keep her warm when he offered her his hand.

"Come on. We're going to take a look around," he said.

She craned her head, taking in the golden field between them and the large redwoods off in the distance. She squinted and was sure she could see a few deer grazing across the meadow. With the sun starting to set, it was gorgeous. Yeah, she wouldn't mind taking her time out there. So what if they got stuck? Surely the Pelshes would notice when the wagon didn't come back, right?

"Okay, but I still want to see your moves on the ice," Georgia said once she was safely on the ground, holding herself up with her crutches.

He raised one eyebrow. "You're not going to let this go, are you?"

She smirked. "What else do I have to poke you about?"

"Okay," he said with a nod. "I'll put on the skates if you promise to try out the sled."

"Sled?" she asked, glancing around. "What am I going to do with that? There's no snow."

"It's a sled for the ice." Logan pointed to the device sitting just inside the shed. "It's meant for people who can't skate but still want to experience the ice."

"You're on," Georgia said excitedly. She loved ice-skating, and while this would in no way enable her to do any of those things, she could at least have a front row seat while watching Logan.

Once Logan had skates on, he stood and wobbled dangerously.

"Whoa," she said, grabbing his arm to steady him. "You need strong ankles. Don't let them loose form, or you're going over for sure."

"I think I need a teacher," he said as he tried to walk over to the ice. He put his arms out to steady himself when his legs started shaking.

"Hey, Logan?" she asked.

"Yeah?"

"When's the last time you did any sort of exercise?" she asked, amused.

"You mean besides carrying you out of the woods?"

She nodded.

"Uh, maybe six months ago? I've been hiking but not doing much else."

"Okay. Well, make sure you have the anti-inflammatories on hand when you get home. Things might get a little sore."

"Noted." He seemed to steady himself, but he stood at the edge of the ice and glanced back at her. "I'm not going until you're on that sled."

"Is that all you're waiting for?" she said, flashing him a smile. "I can make that happen." Georgia crutched over to stand next to him. He had already moved the sled to the edge of the ice and was holding it steady so it wouldn't fly out from under her while she was getting situated. Once she was seated, he carefully pushed it out onto the ice. The sled glided about ten feet and then came to a stop. Georgia crooked her finger at him. "Now you have to come out here, otherwise I'm stuck for good."

"We can't have that." Logan took his first step onto the ice and promptly lost his balance. He fell hard onto the rink, with his feet sticking out over the ice.

"Are you all right?" she asked, her tone full of concern.

"Yeah, just a bruised ego." He pushed himself back up and grabbed the railing that circled the pond. "I'll get it."

"Try using the toe picks. They'll stop you from losing your balance."

Logan stared at his skates as if trying to decipher what in the world toe picks might be.

She pointed to the jagged edge of the blade at the front of his skates.

"Got it." This time when he stepped onto the ice, his legs were shaking again, but he didn't fall.

Georgia held out her hands. "Come over here. You can use me to help balance."

"It's fine, I can—shit!" He wobbled and his arms started to flail.

"Toe pick!" she called.

He lifted one foot and jabbed the toe of the blade into the ice, giving him the stability he needed.

Georgia grinned at him. "See? All your skateboarding reflexes are still there. You can do this."

Determination radiated from his eyes as he concentrated on making his way to Georgia. She wasn't surprised when his legs stopped shaking and he started to glide toward her in an effortless fashion.

"Excellent. Now slow down and—"

"Dammit!" His legs split and Georgia was certain he was going down again, but he reached ahead of him and she grabbed his hands. It was enough to keep him from cracking his tailbone on the ice. "Good catch," he said and nodded his head toward their hands. He was crouched down slightly, while she was sitting on her knees.

"You're the one who reached out for me," she said, smiling up at him. "So, now what? Are you going to pull me around the rink?"

He glanced around, eyeing the twilight, and suddenly he nodded decisively. "You better believe it. I can't pass up this setting, can I?"

"Nope," she said, grinning. "You know, I think I really like this version of you."

"So do I." He clutched her hands and moved backward slowly. When the sled started to move, he grinned at her. "Looks like we're doing it."

"Yes, we are."

As Logan got more comfortable, he picked up the pace a little. Georgia's hair started to move in the breeze, and even though she was on a sled, she decided this was the best ice-skating experience she'd ever had.

"How about we try a spin?" he asked, sounding cocky.

"A spin?" she gasped. "I don't think we're nearly ready for that."

"Relax," he said easily. "I just mean to turn us in a circle so we can head back."

"Oh, sure," she said and was delighted when he turned them with ease.

"Okay, now watch this." Logan slid one skate to the left, putting his entire weight behind it, and the next thing she knew, he was spinning them in a circle.

It was exhilarating with the cool wind in her hair and his hands clutched around hers. She let out a whoop of joy that quickly turned to a cry when Logan's skates slipped out from under him and he went down, pulling her right down on top of him.

They were both silent for a beat as the reality of the moment sank in, then Georgia whispered, "Are you okay?"

"Yeah." Logan reached up and brushed a stray lock of hair out of her eyes. "You?"

She smiled down at him. "Sure. I had a soft landing."

"Good," he whispered. Then he lifted his head and caught her lips with his.

Georgia stiffened for just a second but then relaxed as she sank into the best kiss of her life.

CHAPTER 17

*L*ogan wrapped his arms around Georgia and held her tightly as he deepened the kiss. The magic that always surrounded him when he was holding her intensified and fully consumed him. He didn't even feel the chill from the ice seeping through his clothes. He was all in, unaware of anything other than her soft lips on his.

"Hi," she whispered, pulling back slightly.

"Hey." His voice was hoarse as he stared up at her flushed face.

She pressed a cool palm to his cheek. "This is really nice, but maybe we should get back to the wagon before it gets too cold."

Logan glanced around at their surroundings, noting the sun had already set and they were losing the light. "Yeah, I think you might be right."

Georgia climbed back onto the sled and waited until he got to his feet. He wasn't nearly as wobbly as he was before, but his backside was a little worse for the wear. A slight pain shot down his right leg, but he ignored it as he carefully guided her back to the edge of the pond.

"You're limping," Georgia said a few minutes later from her perch on the wagon.

"Turns out landing flat on your back on the ice isn't recommended," he said, flashing her a small smile. "I'm sure I'll be all right after an anti-inflammatory."

"Maybe we should stop at Charming Herbals. I bet Bree has something that will help."

"It's not that bad," he said and then winced as he hauled himself back into the wagon.

"You don't have to be tough for me." She waved at her foot. "I'm the one who had to be carried out of the woods, remember?"

He chuckled. "You're right. If the shop is open, we'll stop."

"Good. Now let's hope these wheels take us where we need to go." She raised her hands and brought them down quickly as if she were holding reins and said, "Giddyup!"

The wagon lurched forward and then turned around in the clearing.

"Mary told you to do that when we were back at the barn, didn't she?" he asked, eyeing her with suspicion.

"No. I'm just brilliant." She patted his leg and then waved a hand at the trail in front of them. "Look. It's gorgeous."

He followed her gaze and couldn't help but agree. Twinkle lights lit up the trees that lined the trail. Lit pumpkins carved with scenes from the winery floated every ten feet. As if that wasn't enough to set a romantic scene, Frank Sinatra's song, "The Way You Look Tonight," filled the air. He slipped his arm around Georgia and pulled her in until she pressed her head against his shoulder. "This might be the most memorable date I've ever been on."

"It's a date?" she asked, gazing up at him with a small smile.

"If it isn't, then I don't know what is." He tightened his hold on her and settled in to enjoy the rest of the ride.

When they arrived back at the barn, Mary was there to greet them. "Welcome back. I have hot cocoa and gingersnaps waiting."

"Thank you, Mary," Logan said. "You've thought of everything." He climbed down, careful to not move too quickly. Even so, a shot of pain ran down his leg, and he had to bite back a wince.

He turned and reached for Georgia.

Once she was back on the ground and they'd said goodnight to Mary, she narrowed her eyes at him. "You're hurt more than you're letting on."

Damn. She wasn't going to let this go, was she? "I'm fine. I promise."

"No you aren't," she said, shaking her head as she crutched her way toward the SUV.

Logan grabbed the hot cocoa and the gingersnaps. "I said we'd stop at Charming Herbals," he called as he followed her.

"Good." Her expression softened. "Because other than you hurting yourself, today has been perfect."

He opened the door for her. "Want to do it again? Tomorrow afternoon maybe?"

She studied him for a long moment then nodded. "Sure, but let's make it mid-morning and then have a late lunch."

"Are you planning the date even though I asked you out?"

"Yes." She grinned. "There's somewhere I've been wanting to go, and you're the perfect companion."

"Sounds... mysterious." He was dying to know where she wanted to take him, but he held back, enjoying the game.

She shrugged one shoulder. "Not mysterious so much as adventurous."

"Oh, now I'm really curious."

"I bet you are." Georgia turned around, and using her good foot, she hopped up into the seat. "Let's go, Scott Hamilton. There's a hot tub waiting for both of us."

Both of his eyebrows shot up as the image of sharing a bath with her flashed in his mind. "Really? Your place or mine?"

She tossed her head back and laughed. "Okay, I deserved that. But as nice as that sounds, I think that might be moving a little quickly. Sorry, Logan. You're swimming in your tub alone tonight."

He let out an exaggerated sigh. "Your loss."

"No doubt." She took the hot cocoa and cookies from him. "I'll just have to pencil it in on my calendar for another time."

"I'm going to hold you to that." He closed her door and smiled to himself as he hurried around the SUV to the driver's seat.

LOGAN HOBBLED into the healer's office, grimacing from the pain shooting down his leg. The pain reliever he'd gotten from Charming Herbals the night before had certainly numbed the pain, but apparently it had done too good of a job, because he'd slept so soundly he had barely moved all night. That was great right up until the moment he'd tried to get out of bed. That's when everything went to hell. If he didn't get some serious help, his date with Georgia was going to be completely off the table.

"Ah, Mr. Malone," the receptionist said. "Gerry will be right with you."

He stood at the counter and nodded that he'd heard her.

"Go ahead and have a seat," she added.

"I'm fine here." Sitting wasn't an option. He'd barely been able to get out of his SUV, and the only reason he'd made it at all was because Seth had driven him.

The blond receptionist eyed him, nodded once, and then picked up her phone. "Mr. Malone is here. I'd say it's urgent." When she set the phone back on the receiver, she stood. "Let's go, Mr. Malone. Healer Whipple says to send you back."

He let out a relieved sigh, hopeful that he'd be hopped up on pain relievers in no time. Logan took careful steps as he followed the receptionist and was grateful when they finally stopped at an exam room. She opened the door for him and said, "Change into the gown on the bed. When you're ready, just push the button next to the exam table."

Logan struggled to get undressed and into the gown. By the time he was done, he was sweating and muttering curses under his breath. Maybe he should have just gone straight to Charming Herbals. At least the pain potion Bree had given him would've allowed him to breathe without a sharp pain in his back.

There was a knock on his door. When he indicated it was okay to enter, Gerry Whipple poked her head in and smiled at him. "Ready for me?" she asked.

"As ready as I'm gonna be." He was standing next to the exam table because sitting was just too painful.

"Hmm, you look very uncomfortable," she said, already writing something in his chart.

"If you mean because I'm standing here naked in a paper gown, then no. That doesn't bother me. It's the fact that I can barely move, much less sit, without feeling like knives are stabbing me in my spine."

"Oh, dear. That does sound awful." She put her chart down and moved to stand behind him. "Tell me when this started."

"Yesterday. I fell on the ice out at the Pelsh Winery."

"Did you take anything for the pain?" She ran her fingers down his back, pressing the tissue next to his spine very gently.

"Yes, last night. A pain potion from Charming Herbals." He sucked in a sharp breath when she neared the area of his injury.

"Yes, I imagine that does hurt." Her tone was sympathetic and soothing at the same time. "I bet it hurts all the way down to here," she said, pressing his back just above his tailbone.

"Ouch!" he hissed as he flinched and then hissed again.

"Sorry about that," she said. The healer put him through some motions to check his mobility, and when they were done, she leaned against the counter and said, "I can use healing touch to help you heal and prescribe a stronger pain potion, but you're still going to be laid up for a few days."

Logan let out a small groan. "How long is a few days? Three?"

"Yes. Maybe a couple more depending on your progress."

"Damn. I had a date today."

"Sorry about that." She patted his arm, rummaged around in her cabinet, and pulled out a mini bottle of pain potion and a jar of medicinal cream. "Let's get you fixed up so that hopefully you'll be ready to tear up the town in no time."

He put his arms out to the side and said, "Let the healing begin."

Twenty minutes later, Logan had just finished paying and was on his way out when the front door swung open and a tall, dark-haired man strode in, nearly knocking Logan over. "Hey, man. Watch out, will you?"

The man jerked his head up and stared Logan in the eye.

Austin Steele, the man who'd been the other participant in the recent fender bender, was scowling as he said, "Oh, it's you. Is this going to be our thing? A collision every time we meet?"

"Only if you keep cutting me off," he said, giving him the fakest smile he could muster.

"Right." The scowl disappeared as Austin took him in. "Sorry about that. I just have a lot on my mind."

The door to the patient rooms opened, and Brinn, the clerk at Hollow Books, joined them in the lobby. She was busy pulling her long blond hair up into a bun when her gaze landed on Austin, and she froze.

"Brinn?" Austin said, clearly surprised to see her.

"What..." She dropped her hands to her sides and shook her head as if she didn't believe her eyes. "What are you doing here?"

"I have an appointment to see the healer," he said softly, as if he didn't want to scare her away.

"No," she said, raising her voice. "I mean here, in Keating Hollow. You don't belong here anymore, remember?"

His mouth worked, but no words came out, and Logan almost felt bad for the guy. Clearly there was history between the two of them, and Brinn was mad as hell. Brinn started to brush past him when Austin said, "I'm back. For good."

"Oh, really? Well, good for you." There was nothing about her tone that indicated she was happy about that development.

"Brinn," he said, stopping her in her tracks.

"Yes?" She glanced back at him, her expression blank.

He let out a sigh. "I was just going to ask if you know Gideon Alexander."

Logan wondered if he'd been too hasty in refusing to tell Austin where he could find Gideon. He clearly knew Brinn, and it sounded like he'd lived in Keating Hollow before. Maybe he wasn't the outsider Logan had thought.

Brinn frowned. "Why are you looking for Gideon?"

Austin glanced at Logan and then back at her. "It's… I just need to talk to him. I checked his gallery, but they didn't know when he'd be in again."

"He's out of town right now with his partner, Miranda. They left a few days ago."

He blew out a breath. "Any idea when they're coming back?"

"No idea." Brinn caught Logan's eye, gave him a quick wave, and then rushed out the door.

Austin stared after her, looking like a lost puppy, and Logan couldn't help feeling sorry for the guy. He had it bad.

"Good luck, man," Logan said and left the office.

CHAPTER 18

Georgia was on the way out the door when her phone lit up with Logan's name. "Hey," she said. "Can't wait a few more minutes to find out what we're doing? Just wear something casual. Jeans and a T-shirt is fine."

"I've already got the wardrobe down. It's the activity part I'm having issues with," he said.

"Activity?" She paused in front of her door, her key already in the lock. "But you don't even know where we're going."

"If it involves anything other than my recliner or my couch, then I'm afraid it's off limits. Healer Whipple has ordered me to stay off my feet for a few days."

"It's your back, isn't it?" Georgia asked and finished locking her door.

"It is. I could barely move this morning, so I went and got checked out. Sorry, but it looks like I'm going to have to ask for a raincheck."

"That sucks," Georgia said. "I'm sorry you're hurt. How do you feel about visitors? I could return the favor and wait on you hand and foot for a few days." She pulled her car door open, got in, and slammed the door.

"You're already on your way, aren't you?"

Georgia grinned. There was a smile in his voice, and she loved that she was the source of his good mood despite the fact he'd just learned he was regulated to the couch. "Yes. Need me to pick up anything?"

"Cupcakes. And lattes if you're going by Incantation Café."

"On it," she said and ended the call.

SETH OPENED LOGAN'S DOOR, and Georgia held up the bag from Incantation Café. "I come bearing treats."

"You're my hero." He held the door open and gestured for her to come in. "I hope you brought extra. We have three growing boys here."

"Three? Who's the third?" Georgia asked right as her gaze landed on Levi, who was sitting at a baby grand piano and running his fingers over the keys. "Ah, I see."

Levi raised his hand in greeting.

"Did I interrupt something?" she asked, turning and finding Logan resting on his couch. He was propped up with three pillows and had a another one under his knees for support.

"No," he said with a welcoming smile. "Those two were just playing me a song they've been working on."

"Really?" Georgia handed Logan the latte he'd asked for and placed the bag of cupcakes on his table. "Don't stop on my account. Is it the one you were working on yesterday at Magical Notes?"

"No. It's a different one that's not ready yet," Seth said,

taking a seat on the chair across from Logan. "We were getting Logan's input on some lyrics."

"Oh, okay," she said, sinking into the other chair, disappointed. "I suppose I don't like showing my work until it's done either."

"I don't mind," Levi said. "As long as Seth doesn't."

Seth groaned and shook his head. But there was a hint of a smile on his face as he said, "You're so eager."

"Just excited," Levi countered.

"Are you guys working on an album or just messing around?" Georgia asked. "Because that song yesterday was gorgeous."

Seth shrugged. "We started off just messing around, but now? Who knows? We already have one song and are well into another. If this keeps up, maybe we'll record it."

Levi's eyes shone with eagerness. "That would be amazing. Can you imagine me out on tour, singing for thousands of people?"

"Uh-oh, the kid has stars in his eyes," Logan teased and grinned at Georgia.

"No one is touring anything," Seth said as he stood and grabbed an acoustic guitar. "But now that we've spent the last five minutes talking about it, we might as well play it for Georgia."

Georgia clasped her hands together and scooted to the edge of her seat. "I'm ready. Let me have it."

Levi led off with the piano, and after the first few notes, Seth joined in with both the guitar and his low register vocals. The song was the story about a son trying to forgive his father, not for the father's sake, but for the son's. It was even more haunting than the one she'd heard before, and it didn't take long until the tears were streaming down her face.

Levi took over and sang, *"You never knew me, you feared me, and now you'll never see me. I might have found a way to forgive, but I never forget, because you already forced me to pay a debt."*

"Pay a debt," Georgia sang as backup.

Levi nodded his approval, and as he continued to sing, she added her vocals, letting the lyrics wash over her. Her heart was raw when the music faded away, and her eyes were still wet with tears.

"That was… incredible," she choked out, wiping at her eyes.

"Your voice made the difference," Seth said, staring at her with open curiosity. "Why aren't you a vocalist?"

"Me?" Georgia let out a nervous laugh. "I'm not great in front of audiences. I much prefer being behind my keyboard." She glanced at Logan. "Is it the same for you, or did you love the energy of the audiences?"

Logan rubbed his jaw as he considered her question. "In my younger days, I'd have told you I lived for that feedback from the fans. There's an energy that's euphoric. But now? I dunno. I get a little overwhelmed when there are too many people in a room."

"He hates crowds," Seth chimed in. "It didn't used to be that way."

"I suppose I'm just crankier in my old age," Logan joked.

Georgia was certain that wasn't the case. It was likely his traumas had contributed to his need to have a quiet life. She reached over and took his hand in hers, squeezing to let him know she understood. "It's good that we don't all love the spotlight. It leaves more room for people like you two to shine." She pointed at both Levi and Seth. "I can just imagine you two up on stage giving the most amazing concert. I'm gonna need front row seats when it happens."

"Girl," Levi said with a healthy dose of sass. "If I'm up on stage singing this song and you're there, you'll be up on the stage with me. That voice of yours deserves to be heard."

"Thank you," Georgia said, pressing her hands to her warm cheeks. "That's very kind of you."

"Selfish is more like it," Seth added. "The song was good before, but your voice brought it to the next level." He turned his attention to Logan. "You really should see if you can talk her into recording something."

"Georgia knows her own mind," Logan said mildly. "But I'll see what I can do."

"Really? You think you have sway over me?" she teased.

"When it comes to music?" he asked. "Maybe a little."

She didn't bother to deny it. Georgia also felt the magic that sparked when they played together. It would be in those moments when he'd be able to talk her into almost anything. What was interesting was that the magic hadn't been present while she was singing with Levi and Seth. It left no doubt that she and Logan had something special.

"Okay, on that note... Levi?" Seth stood and jerked his head toward the door. "I think it's time to stop intruding on their date."

"You don't have to go," Georgia insisted. "We're just hanging out and having cupcakes."

"I have to get going anyway," Levi said as he stood. "Healer Snow is expecting me this afternoon." Just as he reached for his phone that was lying on the piano, it started playing "Free Fallin'" by Tom Petty. He snatched it up and answered. "Silas, hi. Can I call you right back? I'm just on my way to— What?" His eyes widened, and then a huge grin spread across his face. "Are you serious? That's amazing."

Georgia, Logan, and Seth all were silent as they watched Levi light up with whatever news Silas had given him.

"You deserve this so much, Si. You really do," he said into the phone. There were happy tears standing in his eyes. "Okay, yeah. All right. I'll see you tomorrow. Love you." When he ended the call, he turned to the rest of them and said, "Silas was just nominated for Best Actor for the Oscars. Holy shit!" The color drained from his face suddenly, and he sank back down onto the piano bench. "An Oscar. Do you know what this means?"

Georgia glanced at the other two men. No one had an answer to Levi's question. "No, Levi. What does it mean?"

"He's going to be so busy. The offers will never stop pouring in." He closed his eyes and pressed a hand to his forehead. "It's going to be virtually impossible to see each other."

"But he's coming home tomorrow, right?" Georgia said gently. "To see you."

"And to meet with Cameron. There's a new script he wants to talk to him about. Probably trying to lock him in before everyone else starts calling." Levi covered his face with both hands and let out a frustrated growl before he jerked his head back up. "Gods. Listen to me, worrying about what that means for our time together when I should be ecstatic for him. What kind of boyfriend am I?"

"One that misses his person." Georgia got up and moved to his side. She placed a soft hand on the back of his neck. "It's okay, you know."

He let out a snort of laughter. "What's okay? To be worried about how this great thing that's happening in his life will affect how much I'll see him or if I'll get to see him at all?"

"Yes." She nodded. "It's definitely okay. As long as you're supportive of him, then it's fine to feel whatever you're going to feel. And from what we just heard, you sounded thrilled for him."

"Of course I am. I'm so proud of him. I meant it when I said he deserves this." Levi let out a long breath and looked up, his expression determined. "I just need to get over myself. I'm sure it will work out."

"It will if you want it to," she said.

He let out a soft chuckle. "That's basically what Amelia told me a few months ago. You can't both be wrong, right?"

Georgia nodded her agreement, and when he stood again, she pulled him into a hug and whispered, "It's wonderful that you're so supportive, but I understand what happens when your partner is larger than life. It's easy to find yourself arranging your life to fit theirs. Just make sure you're following *your* dreams while Silas is out chasing his."

He pulled back, met her gaze, and nodded solemnly. "I'll try."

"Good. Now go write some more songs, Levi, because you have one hell of a gift," she said.

"Don't worry," Seth chimed in. "I'm not going to let him off the hook when it comes to writing. We've written two songs in two days. I can't wait to see how deep that well runs."

Levi flushed, and his lips turned up into a tentative smile. "Really?"

"Really." Seth moved to the front door and opened it for Levi. The pair waved and then disappeared outside.

"Well," Georgia said, sitting next to Logan and grabbing the second latte she'd brought but hadn't yet touched. "That was really something."

"*You* were really something," Logan said. "It's a shame you don't have kids. You'd be an excellent mother."

She sputtered through her latte. "What? Me? No way." She

shook her head and let out a self-deprecating laugh. Then she rambled on nervously. "I'd be too caught up in my manuscript and forget to feed them, or pick them up from a friend's house, or even notice if they were killing each other in the next room. Those noise-canceling headphones really do the trick, you know?"

"Relax," he said with a laugh. "I wasn't suggesting anything other than you were really great with Levi. Your nonexistent kids are missing out on a really excellent mom."

"Well, thanks. I think."

"It's definitely a compliment." Logan nodded to the bag on the table. "I hear there's a cupcake or two in there."

She smirked. "That's the rumor."

He reached for the bag, but when he couldn't reach it, she grabbed it for him and asked, "Pumpkin, chocolate, or lemon?"

"Chocolate."

"Typical," she teased and handed it over.

"And your choice is pumpkin, right?" he countered.

"Yep. Always."

"Basic." He winked.

Georgia pulled out her pumpkin muffin. "I'm perfectly find with being called basic." She made a show of taking a big bite and moaned her pleasure.

"I take it back. You're anything but basic," Logan said seriously. "More like magnificent."

Georgia's entire body heated with the compliment, and suddenly she felt shy and awkward sitting in his living room. She averted her gaze, not sure what to say.

The silence weighed heavily between them as they each picked at their cupcakes and sipped their lattes.

Finally, Logan said, "Georgia?"

"Yeah?" she said, still not looking at him.

"Would you mind singing some new lyrics for me while I play this guitar?"

She jerked her head back to stare at him. He was holding a guitar in his lap, and she couldn't help but wonder where it had come from. She hadn't noticed it earlier. "New lyrics? Did you write them?"

He nodded. "They're really rough, but I want to hear what they sound like with this guitar arrangement. And well, I started writing this song with your voice in mind."

Georgia was speechless. "My voice?"

He nodded. "Ever since I heard you sing at the brewery, I just can't get you out of my head."

"I'm not sure how I feel about occupying your mind twenty-four seven."

He rolled his eyes. "I meant your voice, but believe what you want."

"I will." She took a sip of the latte and then set it down on the table. "Okay, I'm ready when you are."

He gazed at her, his silver-gray eyes piercing her, and then he started to play.

CHAPTER 19

*L*ogan wasn't sure what had come over him. It had been years since he'd put the lyrics that rambled in his mind from pen to paper. Hadn't he left that part of himself behind? He blamed Seth and Levi. If they hadn't jumped feet first into working on those songs in front of him, he probably would've been able to put the songwriting aside.

Maybe.

He knew deep down that he was lying to himself. His real downfall was the night he'd helped Georgia out when she sang at the brewery. The fire had been lit, and that was the reason he'd been picking up his guitar so much lately. Logan reached into his pocket and handed Georgia the paper with the lyrics he hadn't been able to get out of his head. He'd titled it "Begin Again."

She held his gaze for a few beats, but then scanned the paper. She sucked in a sharp breath and quickly glanced up at him. "You wrote this?"

He nodded.

"When?"

"Last night." There was no need to tell her he'd written about himself from her perspective. The shock was evident in her dark eyes. He strummed the guitar, almost bursting with the need to play. "Will you sing it for me?"

"Yeah, sure," she whispered, staring at the lyrics again.

"Like I said, they're still rough."

"It's gorgeous," she said firmly. Then she cleared her throat and sat up straight. "Let's do this."

Logan played the first few chords, and when he was ready for her to start, he nodded, giving her the signal.

Her pitch was perfect as she sang the first words in a soft voice. *"It happened that night, I was standing frozen in the spotlight, your fingers on the strings as everyone waited for me to sing."*

Logan held her gaze and brought up the tempo.

Georgia let the song build, adding to the drama. *"You said it was magic. I felt it, too."*

By the time she reached the next section, there was so much emotion in her voice, Logan had to blink back tears. The song was so personal. It put into words everything he'd been terrified to face for the past several years.

"The next day you pulled away, back into your space of dismay. You said you'd already loved and lost. That I'd be better off. But then there was magic, breaking down your wall, making me wonder if it was really safe to fall."

Logan strummed a few more chords on the guitar before stilling his fingers. They both sat there, staring at each other, until finally he said, "Well, what do you think?"

She swallowed hard, and with a determined look on her face, she said, "I think it's time you tell me about your past."

Logan knew this was coming. He never talked about Cherry or Brit. It was just too painful. "I…" He put the guitar aside and prayed for strength. "I know Seth talked to you." His brother had warned him that he'd mentioned she should look up his past. Logan hadn't been pleased that Seth had interfered. But now? If it meant he didn't need to relive those two nights, then he was grateful. "Did you look me up like Seth said?"

Georgia nodded, her gaze full of sympathy.

"So you know about Cherry and Brit," he said, his voice cracking on Cherry's name.

"I know that you lost two people you cared for very much," Georgia said.

"Not just cared for. Cherry... she was in my band, and also my co-writer. We wrote every song together. She was my other half, and then... She died because of me." He gritted his teeth, knowing how dramatic he sounded. It was so cliché to take the blame for what everyone considered an accident. But cliché or not, he was the one who'd begged her to rush to the airport that night. "She didn't want to go with me. The night of the crash, she told me to go alone to the interview. It was storming out and she was tired, not feeling well. But I insisted, telling her I needed her there. She was my partner, the one who lit the magic inside of me. I guilted her into meeting me at the airport, only she never showed."

Georgia didn't say a word, seeming to know that he just needed space to talk.

"You know what the worst part of that effed-up situation was?"

She shook her head.

A dull ache materialized in his chest, something that always happened when he allowed himself to talk about Cherry. "I was pissed when she was late. I thought she was punishing me. I left shitty voice mails on her phone and accused her of trying to tank our chances at making it big." He let out a hollow laugh. "She loved music, but not the music industry. I honestly think she'd have been happy just singing for tips at the local dive bar on the weekends."

"Fame isn't for everyone," Georgia said.

"No. It isn't. And you know what? She was right. I would have hated being famous. I see what Seth goes through, and his band hasn't even cracked the top twenty yet. They have some hits, but they are far from a household name. It's a lot of invasion of privacy and people crossing lines. I suspect if our band had made it really big, I'd have stepped back and ended up in a place like Keating Hollow just to get away from everything."

Georgia smiled at him. "I was here for all of five minutes for a book signing when I realized it was my place. There's just something special about this magical town."

He nodded. "There is. Cherry would've loved it."

"I'm sorry you lost her," Georgia said, taking his hand in both of hers. "I know how it feels to lose someone you love so much. My husband Nick died suddenly in a skiing accident. I thought the pain in my chest would never ease."

"I'm sorry, Georgia. Sorrier than you know," he said, squeezing her hand.

"Thanks. You know how people say time heals all things?"

"I've heard that before." He frowned. "Wish I believed it."

"Yeah. It's bullshit," she confirmed. "You just learn to live with it."

He gave her a sad smile. "I guess it depends on what you mean by living." He shifted slightly so that he could see her better. "I did take a chance on loving again. The connection was instant. Brit and I had this all-consuming passion for each other. It wasn't the partnership that I had with Cherry, but it was real, and I thought I'd finally gotten my second chance at love. Unfortunately, although I do believe that she loved me, she had someone else she was sleeping with the entire time. After I found out about it and told her it was over, she took her own life. I was a mess for a long time after that and convinced myself that love wasn't in the cards for me. That it's too painful. Connections like that... Maybe they're just too bright a flame and are destined to burn out."

Georgia pursed her lips as she studied him. "Are you saying you loved them too much, and that was their ultimate demise?"

He let out a humorless chuckle. "I wouldn't put it quite like that, but yeah. There was a soul-deep magical connection that I felt with each of them. I don't want to say it was love at first sight, because it wasn't. Not with either of them. But there was still magic that ignited when we were together. It was real and undeniable and just about the best feeling in the world. It was easy to swear off love when I hadn't ever felt that with anyone else... until now."

"Until now?" Georgia whispered. Her body had gone completely still while her eyes had widened in pure shock.

"Until now," he confirmed. "It's why I pulled away that night in your room. I keep telling myself it's a bad idea, and then when you told me you were writing scenes that come true, I was certain that this was a terrible idea. Not because I was afraid of what you might write, but because it confirmed that we're linked. Georgia, if we move forward and I lose you, I won't survive it. And more importantly, I'm terrified that something awful will happen to you because of our connection."

Georgia itched to stand. To pace the room. Her foot was starting to become a major inconvenience. Instead, she stared up at the ceiling, contemplating what he'd just said. Finally she looked at him. "That's a lot to take in."

"I know." He swung his legs off the couch and stood, careful not to move too fast. While he was supposed to stay off his feet for a few days, he wasn't an invalid.

"What are you doing?" she asked, placing her hands on her hips. "You know you're supposed to be resting."

"I've been resting all day." He moved to sit on the coffee table right in front of her. Logan cupped her cheeks with his palms and said, "When we play music together, that magic consumes me. I knew that night at the brewery that we were in trouble." He gave her a small smile. "I vowed to keep my distance, but honestly, Georgia, that's a losing battle. Because right now, even with the guitar set aside, that connection is tying us together. I don't think I can fight this, not if you feel it too."

Georgia's eyes searched his. After a few seconds, she shifted forward and said, "Logan, if I say yes, that's going to be it, isn't it?"

He nodded, knowing from experience that he'd never be able to walk away now.

She bit down on her bottom lip before asking, "Would it make a difference if I've already written a scene like this?"

"Have you?" He didn't really think she had. She seemed too surprised by some of his words.

"No." She smiled up at him. "However, I did have plans for the hero to bare his soul to the heroine after she shows him what he'd been missing all the years he was hiding out in the woods. So this is sort of close."

"Does that still freak you out?"

She nodded her head slowly. "It does, but I'm not sure there's anything I can do about it. I either stop writing or stop living. Neither of those options are appealing."

"No, they aren't." He leaned in, giving her plenty of time to pull back.

"Logan, I have to be honest. This relationship we're starting, it's very intense. That connection you talked about, I feel it, too. And I'm sure that if I give myself over to it, if I say yes to pursuing this with you, I'm going to fall hard. I'm not asking for any promises. It's too early for that, but I need to know you're not going to run if it gets hard."

"I can make at least one promise. I won't run," he said thickly.

Georgia had tears in her eyes when she let down her last guard and covered his lips with her own. She wasn't sure how long they stayed locked in each other's arms, but when she finally pulled away, she was breathless and a little dazed. "Whoa."

"I couldn't have said it better myself," he said, caressing her cheek.

She cleared her throat and pulled back, needing a bit of distance. Otherwise, things were going to move at warp speed, and she needed time to process. "What do you say we work on that song some more? Maybe try out some more lyrics?"

His eyes lit up. "Sure. I'd love that." Logan moved back to the couch, settled into a comfortable position, and picked up his guitar, and the two of them spent the next couple of hours turning his song into something deeply personal for both of them.

CHAPTER 20

It had been three days since Georgia had agreed to pursue a relationship with Logan. It had also been three days since she'd seen him. After they'd finished his song that they'd titled "Begin Again," she'd decided it was important for her to go home and give them both time to process what was happening between them.

She sat on the edge of her bed and stared at a photo of her and Nick. It had been taken the summer before his accident. They were at the beach, laughing at something. There was so much joy there. So much love. He'd been her best friend.

The one thing she hadn't had with Nick was that connection she felt with Logan.

She'd be lying if she said her feelings for Logan didn't scare her. It was the reason she'd been the one to pump the brakes. The irony was that she'd done it right after she'd made him promise he wouldn't run.

Georgia ran her fingers over the picture. Where would she be now if Nick had never taken that ski trip? Would they have moved to Keating Hollow together? She really didn't think so.

He'd loved the city and the beach down in Southern California. And Georgia just knew he'd have balked at the idea of small-town life.

Sighing, she stood, crutched her way over to her bookcase, and placed the photo on one of the shelves.

As hard as it was to admit it, she'd compromised more than she was really comfortable with when she'd been married to Nick. Georgia had often considered his wants and needs before hers, and it took being on her own to realize just how often she'd ignored what she wanted in an effort to avoid conflict. She refused to repeat that mistake going forward in any relationship.

And that, more than anything, was why she needed a little space from Logan. She liked being on her own. Not answering to anyone. Living her life on her own terms. She hadn't even been looking to date anyone, not seriously anyway, and then Logan walked into her life.

Logan had the power to change everything. It would be so easy to get lost in him. But that was the one thing she refused to do.

Georgia was happy to share her life, her heart, and her love, but she did not want to find herself living someone else's dream. She'd been there, done that. Now it was her turn to prioritize herself.

Her phone buzzed with a text. She smiled when she saw it was from Logan.

I'm leaving in ten. Are jeans and a T-shirt still the dress code?

Georgia smiled to herself as she returned his text. *And comfortable shoes.*

Is there any other kind? He finished the text with a heart emoji.

Georgia stuffed her phone in her pocket and crutched her way downstairs.

~

"OKAY, where exactly are we going where you're going to be on crutches that I need comfortable shoes?" Logan asked as Georgia steered her car down the highway toward the ocean.

"You'll see." She grinned at him. "You're going to love it."

"Fine. Don't tell me." He turned in his seat, his gaze boring into her.

"What?" she asked, side-eyeing him. He was acting a little cagey, like he had something he wanted to tell her but hadn't quite decided he was ready. "Something's up."

Logan let out a low chuckle. "There's no getting anything by you, is there?"

"Nope. Spill." She turned her attention back to the road, concentrating on the winding highway.

"So, remember when you got to my house a few days ago and Seth and Levi were there working on a song?" he asked.

"Sure. They sounded great. Did they finish it?"

"Yes, they did as a matter of fact. Those two have been spending all their free time together working on ideas. I swear, if they keep this up, they'll be ready to record an album by the end of the month. As it is, they're putting together a demo to send to Seth's record label."

"That's exciting." Georgia glanced over at him with a small frown of confusion. "But what about Seth's band? Aren't they still together?"

"Technically they are, but they can't do anything unless Cal comes back. They can't make music or tour since Cal is their lead singer. He's not even talking to Seth, so Seth has no idea how things are going to go down, but he's anticipating the band breaking up. The label will throw a fit, but since Seth has always been willing to fulfill his obligations, he won't be the one in breach of contract. It'll be Cal who will get sued by everyone unless an agreement can be worked out."

"That sounds messy and complicated," Georgia said as she made a left turn onto Highway 101, heading south toward Eureka.

"It is. But Seth's doing what he does best and channeling his emotions into his music."

"Good for him. And Levi, too, it sounds like."

Logan nodded. "Yeah, and this is where we come in."

Georgia raised both eyebrows. "We? What does that mean?"

"Glad you asked." He gave her a cheeky grin. "Back to that day when Levi and Seth were working in my living room. They were actually recording their session and forgot to stop the recorder when they left."

"They what?" Georgia felt her entire body go cold. "Does that mean our entire conversation was recorded? Oh my gods, did they listen to our private discussion?" While they hadn't said anything that would end up on a gossip website, she didn't love the idea of anyone else being privy to their private life.

"Oh, no! I found it after you left and deleted everything except the song. You sound wonderful, Georgia."

Pleasure wound through her from his praise. "Thanks. I guess it's nice that we caught it on tape."

"It gets better. Seth heard it, and he wants us to record it."

"Record it?" Georgia was busy trying to find a parking spot and decided she hadn't heard him correctly. Once she had the car parked in a large parking lot near the beach, she turned to him. "What do you mean, record it? Didn't we already do that if you have it on tape?"

"I meant record it in the studio. Seth says it's the kind of thing his label is looking for, and we could have a shot at getting it published."

While Georgia was a writer, she didn't really know much about the world of music, and she had questions. "What does it mean to have a song published?"

"We'd make a demo and then have the label send it out to producers to see who'd be interested in recording it. If it's picked up, we'd get songwriting credit and royalties once it's published."

"I'd love to do that!" Georgia got butterflies in her stomach thinking about it. How cool would it be to hear someone amazing singing their song on the radio? "When does he want us to do that?"

"He has some studio time later this week. So you're in?"

"I'm in."

They grinned excitedly at each other.

Then Logan glanced around and said, "Did you bring me to a carnival?"

"Not just a carnival," she said. "A beachside carnival. It's all part of my plan to make you see Keating Hollow isn't just about the hiking trails."

"But we're not in Keating Hollow," he teased.

"Close enough." She pushed her door open. "Come on, buddy. There's a Ferris wheel with my name on it."

Logan didn't waste any time rushing to her side of the car. Apparently he was over his ice-skating injury. He held a hand out to her, helping her steady herself as she used both him and one of her crutches to haul herself out of the seat. Once she had both crutches and was balancing comfortably by his side, he said, "I'm game for the carnival if you are, but are you sure you want to crutch around the place?"

"Oh, I won't be crutching." She winked. "Just follow me."

Logan didn't question. He just let her take the lead and remained ready in case she needed anything.

Once they got to the entrance of the park, a woman in a blue uniform wheeled a chair over to her and said, "Ms. Exler? I'm Jean. I believe we spoke on the phone?"

"Yes, that's me." Georgia beamed at her. "Thank you for this. My boyfriend was concerned about how I was going to get around." *Boyfriend.* The word ping-ponged around in her mind. It was the first time she'd allowed herself to use it, and it felt good. Damned good. She winked at him.

He winked back, looking sexy in his faded jeans and open flannel button down over his white T-shirt.

Once Georgia was in the chair, the woman took the crutches and waved to an office behind her. "When you're ready to go, just come right back here to the office. I'll have your crutches waiting for you."

"Thank you, Jean." Georgia nodded to Logan. "Let's roll."

Logan moved behind her, leaned down and said, "Does this mean once we get our tickets we can go to the front of every line?"

"Yep." She glanced over her shoulder. "It's the perfect time to come, right? Another week and we'd be the suckers at the end of the line."

They both laughed as Logan guided her through the crowd of people eating cotton candy and fried Twinkies.

Three hours later, Georgia pressed her hand to her stomach and groaned. "I can't eat one more thing."

"Not even a funnel cake?" Logan asked, pointing to the line in front of them. "Fried dough covered in powdered sugar looks amazing."

Her stomach rolled at the thought. "No way. Not unless you want me to yak in the car on the way back."

Logan laughed. "No, thanks. I think we're done here."

"But we haven't ridden the Ferris wheel yet," she protested. "I was saving the best for last."

He gave her a skeptical glance. "Really? You just said you might yak in the car."

"Only if I keep eating." She glanced over at the ride. "Look, the line isn't even very long."

"Like that matters. That wheel chair is magic."

That was true. They hadn't waited more than five minutes for any ride in the park. "Okay, fine. How about if I promise you we can make out at the top."

"You're on." He immediately started pushing her chair toward the ride while Georgia laughed.

"You're too easy," she said.

"I beg to differ. You're the one who's throwing herself at me," he teased.

"Georgia? Logan?" a familiar voice called from right behind them.

Logan stopped, and they both craned their necks to find Miranda Moon and Gideon Alexander walking toward them hand-in-hand.

"Miranda! What are you two doing here? I thought you were out of town," Georgia said, grabbing the wheels and turning around to greet her friend.

"We were, sort of. We spent the last few weeks exploring the coast. We're headed back to town tonight." Her gaze focused on Georgia's foot. "What happened?"

"Hiking incident. It's fine. I just can't put any weight on it for another week or so," Georgia said.

"So naturally you came to the carnival," Gideon chimed in.

"Hey, man. It's the best time to come," Logan added. "We haven't waited in a single line."

"Nice." Miranda nodded in approval, then she slid her gaze from Georgia to Logan and back again. There was a knowing look in her eyes, and Georgia knew she'd be grilled later. That was fine. She could use a little dish time with a friend.

"We're headed to the Ferris wheel," Georgia said. "You two interested?"

"Is that even a real question?" Miranda asked, slipping her arm through Gideon's. "Lead on."

Once they were waiting for the Ferris wheel to finish unloading, Gideon stepped up to stand beside Logan. "Hey. How's the new book coming? Any progress?"

Georgia watched their interaction with interest. She didn't know that Logan was friendly with Gideon. In fact, other than when he was with her, she hadn't seen him with anyone other than Seth and Levi. But they clearly were familiar enough for Gideon to know Logan had started a new book.

"It's not," Logan said with an unconcerned shrug. "My brother's in town, and he's been working on new music."

"That's got to be distracting," Gideon said.

"He's loving it," Georgia chimed in. "He's been playing and writing a bit, too."

"Really?" Gideon seemed impressed. "Music, huh? That's cool. I can't wait to hear some of it."

"Me, too," Miranda said. "I'd love to hear it, maybe see if any of it is a good fit for a guest appearance on the new series Cameron and I just sold."

"You sold another series!" Georgia cried. "That's incredible. That's the second one, right?"

She nodded. "It's set in a small town, not unlike Keating Hollow, but everyone has a different ability. It has a lot of

Buffy vibes, minus the Hellmouth. Cool, hip, teenage drama, only make it urban fantasy. That's how we pitched it anyway."

"So good," Georgia gushed. "I'm standing… er sitting here in the presence of greatness. I'm blown away."

"Stop," Miranda said, her cheeks flushing. "We just got lucky, that's all."

"No you didn't," Gideon said, nudging her a little bit. "You worked hard for this. It wasn't lucky. If anything, it's persistence."

"Listen to the man, Miranda," Georgia said. "He's right. It wasn't luck. You and Cameron made that happen. And can I just say how damned thrilled I am for you?" Georgia held her arms up, reaching for her friend to give her a hug.

"Thanks, Miranda," Logan said. "I'll remember to have Seth send the demo over."

"You do that," she said.

The ride operator waved to them to indicate it was their turn to get on the ride.

"Time to kiss the clouds," Logan said, pushing Georgia forward.

She glanced back. "If we don't see you after, it was nice seeing you. And call me, we'll get together for drinks one night soon."

"We're looking forward to it," Miranda called back.

"Oh, hey, Gideon?" Logan called.

"Yeah?"

"I forgot to tell you. There's a man in town looking for you. Someone named Austin Steele. He wanted me to give him your address. I refused, but he does know where your shop is, so you'll probably run into him sooner than later."

Gideon furrowed his brow and shook his head. "That name

doesn't—wait. It does sound familiar." He turned to Miranda. "Ring any bells?"

"Not a one," she said

"I guess if he knows where my shop is, I'll find out what he wants soon enough. Thanks for the heads-up, Logan. I appreciate it."

"Of course. What else are neighbors for?" They did a complicated handshake, causing the ride operator to lose his patience.

"Are you getting on or not?" the operator barked. "Just because she can't walk, that doesn't mean you can hold up the line for forever."

"Sorry!" Georgia called and elbowed Logan in the thigh. "Come on. Last call for making out at the top." Georgia heard Miranda and Gideon chuckling as Logan wheeled her off for the Ferris wheel fantasy she'd been dreaming about since she was a teenager.

CHAPTER 21

The next week was heaven as far as Logan was concerned. He'd spent nearly every day with Georgia since the date they'd had at the carnival. They'd come home with stomachaches, a couple of stuffed bears from the game booths, and a selfie photo of them kissing at the top of the Ferris wheel. It had been the perfect day.

So had the day Georgia had insisted on them both taking a baking class that Miss Maple offered in her back room. Georgia had made a cheesecake, and he'd made doughnuts. The cheesecake came out perfect. The doughnuts... Well, they needed work. But he'd still had a blast. Then there was the book fair, the farmers' market, Hard Cider Friday, and a special premier of Silas's new movie at Cameron and Wanda's house. Silas had been so gracious to show up and answer questions. It had been a night to remember.

To say that Logan was enjoying his time with Georgia exploring Keating Hollow would be an understatement. In fact, he couldn't remember a time when he'd been happier.

Georgia had really gone out of her way to show him what she loved about the town. With her by his side, he'd fallen even deeper in love with the place he'd decided to call home.

"I'm nervous," Georgia said. She was finally off her crutches and was standing in front of him, fidgeting. Why was she fidgeting? That wasn't something he'd ever seen her do before.

"About what? Seth and Levi have already heard you sing," he said.

"I know, but that was just messing around. This is... important to you." She walked over to the window that looked into the sound engineer's booth. "Look." She pointed at it. "This is professional, not some low-tech recorder that's just sitting in the middle of the room."

"It's only semi-professional," Chad said, walking into the rented space with Seth, Levi, and Silas behind him. "It's not what you'd find at a record company, but it will do for what we need."

When Seth and Levi decided they were going to lay down tracks for the record company, they'd enlisted Chad to help them find a place to do it somewhere around Keating Hollow. With Wanda's help, they'd been surprised to find a property in town that had been used for a radio station that had gone defunct about ten years back, and it already had a sound-proof booth. Wanda had worked some magic to get them a three-month lease, and they'd gotten right to work on making it suitable for recording. After cleaning it out, they'd outfitted the space with updated equipment. And now here they all were, ready to record new music.

Chad walked over to the keyboards and gestured for Levi, Seth, and Logan to take their places. "Let's warm up a little while we're waiting for our sound guy to get ready."

The sound guy was none other than Silas Ansell. It turned out that he'd had an interest in mixing music when he was younger and had spent a lot of time in a recording studio with a friend of his, learning some things while also having the added benefit of avoiding his controlling stage mom.

When Silas disappeared into the sound room, Logan sat behind the drums, watching Georgia. It seemed there was something more than nerves bothering her, but he couldn't be sure. She'd definitely wanted to come to the studio to work on their song, but the moment she'd stepped inside, she started to look a little green around the gills.

While Levi and Chad warmed up on their instruments, Logan made his way over to Georgia and placed his hands on her shoulders. "Are you sure you're okay? You look like you did after you ate that last fried Twinkie."

"Oh, gods," she cried and buried her head in his shoulder. "Don't bring that up. I really will yak." She held on and pressed closer to him. "I'm just really nervous. I don't know why. Maybe because I know important music people could hear this. I don't want to sound like one of those delusional people who try out for "American Idol" without a clue they can't sing."

"You definitely will not sound like that," he said with a chuckle. "Trust me, babe. You'd blow that competition away if you tried out."

"I'm too old. They wouldn't take me," she muttered.

"Their loss." He ran a hand over her dark curls, trying to sooth her. "Trust me, okay? We won't let anyone hear anything that's not amazing. You'll have veto power. Does that work?"

She nodded, still not letting him go, but her pulse had started to return to normal, and the dread in the pit of her stomach had eased. "It really is a great song, isn't it?"

"It is. And when you sing it, you sound like an angel," he confirmed.

"Okay, is everyone just about ready?" Silas asked through the intercom. "'Cause I'm ready to go in here."

Logan glanced down at Georgia. "Are you ready?"

"No," she said with a chuckle. "But then again, I doubt I'll ever be. Let's get this show on the road."

"Let's hit it boys," Logan said, making his way back to the drums. "Our girl is ready to tear our hearts out."

"On four," Seth said. "One, two, three, four."

The arrangement had changed a bit to accommodate the band, but the intro was still that heartbreaking melody that moved Logan in a way that most music couldn't. He was transfixed, watching Georgia. The moment the music started, he visibly noted her shoulders relaxing and the music winding through her. He just knew she was going to be spectacular. He could feel it all the way to his toes.

And when she opened her mouth and sang their words, his heart burst right open in his chest. He knew he could listen to her do this for the rest of his life. There was no doubt in his mind that if she wanted a career as a recording artist, she'd be snatched up instantly. She had that Adele quality that made everyone just stop what they were doing when they heard her.

Georgia's eyes were closed, but her body moved with each note, telling its own story of love and second chances. Her authenticity drew him in, leaving him transfixed by every one of her movements. Every note. Every breath.

When the music finally died out, the band was uncharacteristically quiet. Georgia glanced around, acting as if she were waiting for a verdict. When it didn't come, her elated expression fell to one of concern.

Logan jumped up off his drum seat and started to clap.

Seth, Levi, and Chad all joined in, with some of them hooting and hollering their approval.

A chuckle came over the intercom. "That was really great," Silas said. "Now can we try it as a duet? I think it might be more powerful if the words are delivered from two different perspectives."

"Yeah, sure," Logan said as he pulled out a sheet of paper that had the song lyrics written out. He quickly made some changes, showed them to Georgia, and then let Levi have the drums. Because Logan had a song to sing.

"You did fantastic," Logan whispered to her. "This is just so they have options."

"Sure. It's fine." Georgia slipped her hand into his, and he squeezed her fingers for support.

"Let me know if any of this is too much. If so, we can always cut it short," he offered.

But Georgia just glared at him and shook her head in irritation. "I'm not that delicate, Logan. Stop treating me like I'm made of glass. I can do this. Now, let's give these guys a show to remember."

"You're on," he agreed.

This time when the music started, Logan kept his gaze locked firmly on Georgia. The familiar magic was there, only tenfold stronger. All he saw was her as they told their story to each other. He was transfixed to the point that even the band and the notes had disappeared. All that was left was the two of them and the love sparking between them.

When both of their voices faded away, Logan stood still, staring down at her in awe. She held his gaze, looking radiant as she glowed with happiness.

"That's it," Silas said through the intercom. "We've got it."

The room erupted with applause and whistles as the other men demonstrated their approval.

"I think they liked it," Georgia said, still clutching Logan.

"Of course they did," Logan said. Because he knew all the way down to the bottom of his soul that they'd just made a hit record.

CHAPTER 22

Georgia sat at her desk, staring at the blank page in front of her. She'd spent the last few weeks writing scene after scene of her hero and heroine getting closer. The hero had started to open up, and her heroine was starting to trust that her shifter was going to stay with her. That he wouldn't suddenly leave and disappear back into the woods to deal with issues from his former pack. They were happy.

She wondered if she could just write the epilogue. If she could just avoid the so-called black moment altogether. Her notebook was open to the page where she'd written: *Black moment. The hero's past comes back to haunt him.*

The scene was already playing out in her head. The hero was on his way to pick up his date. It was the night he was going to declare his love for her. He had a signed copy of her favorite book, keys to a new place he'd just purchased on the side of the mountaintop, and a promise to love her forever. He intended to ask her how she felt about wolf pups and if she thought they might be in her future. It was the happy ending he didn't think he'd ever get or deserve.

But before he gets to her house, he runs over something, causing a flat tire. When he gets out, wolves surround him. They are members of his old pack. They come with devastating news that the pack is in trouble and they need his help. He has to choose; the pack and everything he's ever known or starting a new life with the one who has his heart. Loyalty to his pack wins, and he disappears.

"Ugh!" Georgia stood abruptly, refusing to write the scene that was so clear in her mind. Maybe if she didn't put it into words, she wouldn't have to live through losing Logan.

Her stomach churned, and tears welled in her eyes. Why was this happening to her? She'd lived nearly four decades without even a whisper of magical talent. That fact had frustrated her a lot in her younger days. Growing up surrounded by witches when she couldn't even master an herbal potion had been a blow to her self-esteem as a younger person. But she'd gotten over it. Learned to love who she was. Now? She wanted to give this curse back. Knowing what was coming just sucked.

She picked up the phone and called her aunt Dee.

Dee answered immediately. "Georgia, what a lovely surprise. You almost never call during working hours. Are you having trouble with the book?"

"Yes," she answered and then immediately said, "No."

Her aunt chuckled. "Sounds like you could use an ear."

"I can't finish the book," Georgia said. "Almost every chapter has come true. Or at least, it's been close enough that I've lived through the same emotional pain and growth as my heroine. Now I have to write the moment when the hero leaves her, and I just can't do it."

"So don't," Dee said. "Write the ending you want. No one ever said tragedy has to happen before the dawn."

"Yes, they have. Haven't you ever read a plotting book?" she asked her aunt, already knowing the answer was no. Her aunt wasn't an author.

"I just meant that you can make your own rules. No one is stopping you," Dee said. "It's not like you have a publisher to answer to."

"That's true." Georgia started to calm down. "Maybe I can do some other sort of resolution to wrap this up."

"There you go. Now don't you feel better?"

"Maybe? I just want this book done so I can't stop worrying about how it's going to affect my relationship." Georgia moved to her window and stared out at the redwoods behind her house. "I suppose a walk in the woods might help me brainstorm some ideas."

"How about a day at the spa," Dee said. "That always helps me. Massage, seaweed wrap, facial, mani-pedi. How about I call up the spa there in town and get you set up with the works. If I can't be there, then I can at least spoil you from afar."

Georgia laughed at her aunt. "You know you don't have to do that."

"It's not a matter of having to do anything, sweetie pie. It's a matter of your auntie wanting to. Now let me get off this phone. I have an appointment to make for you. I'll text you when it's done."

"I love you," Georgia said, feeling a thousand times better. It wasn't because her aunt decided to give her a spa day, though that certainly didn't hurt. It was because Dee had made her feel better by just being there for her. "You should come visit soon."

"I will, dear. Don't worry. I'm not going to miss all the festivities."

"What festivities?" Georgia asked. "You mean the holidays?" Christmas in Keating Hollow was always wonderful, though it was nothing compared to Christmas Grove, a town a few hours away that was pure magic all the time.

"Sure. The holidays. Gotta run. Love you." Dee clicked off the call and Georgia sat back down at her desk.

Instead of writing the next scene, Georgia jotted down some notes, trying to put her aunt's advice into action. Maybe she'd have the hero try to work through his issues with a normal life before he could get together with the heroine. Instead of living free as a wolf, he'd try to get a nine to five job, wear a suit, and volunteer at the town fire station. Maybe he'd find out he needs to be true to himself before he can commit to his heroine.

Yes, she thought. That could work. It meant a significant revision, but it wouldn't be the first time or the last. It was time to dig in.

～

"GEORGIA, Hope is ready for you now," Lena, the petite receptionist at A Touch of Magic, called. "You can go right on back. She'll meet you just inside."

"Thanks, Lena." Georgia made a note to book another appointment on the way out. She was always meaning to make massages a regular part of her self-care, but she always forgot to prioritize herself when she was on deadline. No more, she promised herself. She'd just make it a regular thing. Like dental appointments. Only enjoyable.

Hope Garber, her massage therapist of choice, was waiting

for Georgia just on the other side of the door. "Hey. Long time no see," she said with a genuine smile. "I hear you've been busy."

"Aren't we all?" Georgia said, not wanting to talk about her book. She was there to relax, not worry about the missing scenes she still needed to write. "What about you? Business good?"

"Couldn't be better," she said. "In fact, it looks like we're going to need to start hiring again. We're busier than ever, and now that Faith is having triplets, she's not going to be around much. It's a lot, but I'm happy to take on a larger role so she can spend time with her family."

"I still can't get over the triplets thing," Georgia said. "I can't even imagine one baby, let alone three."

"You and me both!" Hope opened a door and ushered her into one of the private rooms. "Chad and I are talking about fostering. Since Levi and I had such an awful time growing up, I really want to turn my home into a haven for someone who really needs one."

"That's amazing," Georgia said, admiring her. She herself hadn't given much thought to having kids. That hadn't ever been one of her plans, but she imagined fostering, while challenging, would be very rewarding in the end.

"We're still in the talking phase." Hope smiled. "But now that it looks like Levi is going to be spending a good amount of time in LA for the next year or so, we'll probably get more serious about it. I'll miss having a teenager in the house."

Georgia was in the process of hanging her coat and purse on the wall pegs, and she nearly dropped them both at Hope's revelation. When she turned around, she asked, "What do you mean Levi is going to be in LA? Is he going down there to spend time with Silas?"

"Silas?" She frowned. "No. Silas is filming up in Vancouver over the next several months. Levi is going down with Seth to record an album. Didn't Logan tell you that Seth's label is fawning all over them? They want to sign them as a duo."

Georgia shook her head slowly and wondered why Logan hadn't called. But then she realized she'd told him she needed to get her book done. Maybe he was saving the news for later. "That's really amazing, Hope. Levi is so talented. I was amazed when I heard a couple of songs he was working on with Seth."

"Right? I honestly had no idea he had that kind of talent. How did I not know he had such an angelic singing voice?"

"I heard he was hiding it in the shower," Georgia said.

"I guess so." Hope beamed as she added, "Chad said he was a quick study on the drums and the piano. So it seems like maybe this is his calling. At least for now. It means giving up his internship with Healer Snow, but she's being really amazing about it. Said he can pick back up whenever he wants to. That his talent wasn't going to fade. I'm just so overjoyed for him and how far he's come." She clutched her fist to her chest. "He really does make a sister proud."

"You have every reason to be proud. He's a great kid. And no matter where he ends up in his career choices, I'm sure he's going to rock it."

Hope chuckled. "Yeah. He will. And then he and Silas really will be one hell of a power couple. Can you imagine? Movie star and rock star? They'll have the world at their feet."

Georgia nodded. It was exciting to think about Levi making it big in the music business. He had the personality for it. Grounded, dedicated, and a solid family behind him for support. She just hoped he didn't get caught up in all the glamour of it. Or worn down by the crush of people who'd want something from him. Georgia wouldn't last two weeks in that sort of situation. Still, she was ecstatic for him. "Just wait, in a few years he and Silas will be labeled as the sexiest men alive. And you'll have to see your half-naked brother on the cover of a magazine or twelve."

Groaning, Hope pressed her hand to her eyes. "Thanks for that visual. Now I need brain bleach."

They were both still chuckling as Hope left the room so Georgia could get ready for her massage. Ten minutes later, all thoughts of music deals, deadlines, and magazine covers had fled. The only thing that mattered in that moment was Hope's magical touch easing Georgia's pent-up tension.

CHAPTER 23

*L*ogan bounced up onto Georgia's porch. He'd been dying to call her, to tell her everything that had gone down in the last two days, but he knew she was trying to finish her book. He'd been there too many times to count and didn't want to distract her.

But she'd called and asked him to dinner, so tonight was the night he was going to surprise her with the great news.

The door opened before he could even knock, and Georgia stood there in ripped jeans and a red-wine colored velvet top. Her skin was radiant and she practically glowed.

"Wow. You look lovely this evening," he said, leaning in to kiss her on the cheek.

"Thanks. You don't look too bad yourself." She moved aside, inviting him in.

Logan was wearing black jeans, a cream sweater, and black boots. It was his go-to date outfit. The scent of basil and rosemary permeated the air, making Logan's stomach rumble with anticipation. "It smells wonderful in here."

"Thanks. There's Tuscany seafood stew on the stove and garlic bread in the oven."

"You cooked? Does that mean the book is done?" he asked, ready to congratulate her.

"Ah, no. But I did make some serious progress. There's just one section I need to work out." She led the way to the kitchen in the back of the house where she had two wine glasses waiting. She grabbed them both and handed one to Logan. "Here."

He took it, held the glass up, and said, "To what comes next."

Georgia eyed him for a moment as if trying to decide what he was referring to, but then she relaxed and touched her glass to his. "To what comes next."

Their eyes locked as they each sipped the merlot.

Logan was so enthralled with her, he set his glass down and moved in, wrapping his arms around her waist and pulling her in close. "I missed you the last couple of days."

Her lips curved into a pleased smile. "You did? Why didn't you call?"

"I didn't want to interrupt. I know how I am when I'm trying to finish a book. I figured you'd call me when you were ready to emerge from your office." Logan felt her body relax under his touch as she leaned into him.

"What did I do to get so lucky? No one ever understands that part of the process. Only other writers."

"It's a first for me, too." He tucked one of her stray dark curls behind her ear. "Thank you for making dinner. I'm sure it's delicious."

She chuckled. "You might want to reserve judgment until you taste it. I haven't cooked anything in ages."

"How about I start here." He bent his head and pressed his

lips to hers. When she opened for him, he deepened the kiss, tasting the merlot on her tongue. Her hands slid slowly up his back, until one hand tangled in his hair. He loved the way she made him feel completely alive when she was touching him. And he wanted her hands everywhere.

"Logan?" she murmured.

"Hmm?" He took the opportunity to kiss his way down her neck, loving the way she shuddered when he nipped at her pulse.

Her hands clutched him tighter and her breath quickened.

Logan smiled against her skin and ran his own hands down along her curves. "Suddenly, I think I'm hungry for a lot more than dinner."

Georgia stiffened and pulled back.

He frowned as he stared down at her swollen lips and flushed cheeks. "Is everything okay?"

"Yeah, I..." She ran a hand over her mussed curls and let out a nervous chuckle. "I wasn't expecting the evening to move quite this quickly."

"Right." He took a step back and willed his libido to calm the eff down. He wanted her desperately. It didn't help that every night for the past week, he'd been dreaming about her gorgeous body, her soft lips, and the little noises she made when she was turned on. "Sorry. Perhaps I'm a little too eager."

"Make that two of us." Her lips quirked up into a half smile. "But dinner's ready, and I want to catch up a little."

"You're right." He sighed and grabbed his wine glass again. "Is there anything I can help with?"

"Sure. Dish out the stew, and I'll deal with the bread."

Once they had dinner on the table and refills on their wine, Georgia sat across from Logan and said, "So, tell me what you've been up to the last few days."

"Thinking about you," he said with a cheeky grin.

Georgia rolled her eyes but couldn't help smiling. She liked his flirty side. "Okay, what else have you been doing?"

He took a long sip of his wine. "It's been a really interesting week."

"So I've heard," she said, narrowing her eyes at him.

His mouth dropped open in surprise. "You heard? What did you hear?"

"Something about a recording contract." She leaned forward, propping her elbows on the table.

He let out a long breath. "Well, someone spoiled the surprise. Who was it? Seth? Levi?"

"Hope. I went to the spa today." She gave him a self-satisfied smile.

"Hope," he said, leaning back in his chair and looking relieved. "She told you about Levi and Seth?"

"Yeah, that Seth's label wants to sign them and record an album. Why didn't you tell me right away?" she demanded, her excitement for Levi and Seth getting the better of her. She was grinning ear to ear when she added, "That's amazing. Levi must be going out of his mind. Just a few weeks ago he was messing around at Magical Notes, and now a fancy label wants him. How did it happen? Tell me everything."

Logan laughed, his eyes sparkling with amusement. "Well, Seth got on the phone with his rep at the label and told them what he's been up to. They wanted to hear the new work, so he sent it over. Within two hours, they called him back and wanted to talk business."

"Wow, so they love it then. Seth must be over the moon."

"They do." He leaned forward, matching her posture. "And here's the thing. They told Seth if he and Levi sign as a new act, they'll let him out of his contract with Lost Pearl. It turns out that Cal is refusing to go back if Seth is there. The label is tired of fighting him and think it's better if they just do a work around. They see this as a win-win for them. Seth will get to keep playing "The One" on tour, so it will help launch him and Levi as a new act. Now the label will have two successful acts instead of one and a whole lot less drama."

"Whoa." Georgia grabbed her wine and took a drink. "That's quite the plan. How does Seth feel about it?"

"Good. He's tired of the drama and just wants to play. And since he's really enjoying the collaboration with Levi, he jumped at the chance. They're flying down at the end of the week to sign the contracts."

"Wow. That's fast. They aren't dragging their feet on this, are they?" Georgia asked.

"No. I guess Lost Pearl has some tour dates they don't want to cancel. If they can get this deal done, they can get Cal back on board and push on without refunding most of the tickets."

"It's always about the money, isn't it," Georgia said, shaking her head. "But if it works in Seth and Levi's favor, then I'm happy for them."

Logan nodded and took a moment to taste the seafood stew. "Yum," he said as he made a face of pure satisfaction. "This is really incredible."

"Thank you." Georgia dipped her spoon and was about to take a bite when Logan cleared his throat. She raised her eyebrows, waiting to hear whatever he wanted to say.

He shifted nervously in his chair. "What are you doing this weekend?"

"Well, I was hoping my boyfriend would want to go do something fun. There's a Fall Fest at the Pelsh Winery. Lots of artists are supposed to be there. I also heard talk about some golf cart races to raise money for the Christmas Festival. Or—"

"How about a movie premiere?" he asked, cutting her off.

"A movie premiere?" she parroted as if she hadn't heard him.

"Yeah. Seth's label was responsible for the original music and offered us tickets. It's called *First Note*, I think." Logan was clutching his wine glass, looking more nervous than ever.

"Tickets for *us*?" she asked, unable to understand why the label was pulling out the stops for Seth's brother and his girlfriend. "How did we luck into those?"

"It turns out when Seth sent his and Levi's new music to the label, he also sent the song we recorded. And they've offered us a publishing deal."

Georgia blinked at him, certain she'd heard him wrong. "What did you just say?"

"The label loves our song. They want to sign us to write more."

"You're kidding." She sat back, completely stunned. "How did this happen? I've only ever written the one song, Logan. Surely they don't want me after only hearing one song."

"Georgia. They're a big record label. You don't think they've done their research? They know you're a successful writer. Of course they want to snatch you up before someone else does. Plus, they know my history as a former musician. The contract is very generous to us. We get to write whenever we want, and they broker the deals with the artists who want them. No real pressure."

"That's... this can't be real," she said. "We work on songs in our spare time, and we have someone to shop them for us?"

"That's pretty much it," he confirmed. "So, are you free this weekend? The premiere is Friday night. We'd leave in the morning."

"Yes!" She jumped up, ran over to him, and sat in his lap as she wrapped her arms around him. Their lips met, and Georgia let go of every reservation she'd ever had. Her hands were in his hair, while he had one on her thigh and another at the nape of her neck. It wasn't enough. She wanted to feel all of him and for him to feel all of her. When she broke off the kiss, she said, "I want you."

He was breathless when he echoed her words back to her. "I want you."

"Good." Georgia stood and held her hand out to him.

He glanced at the food on the table. "Should we clean up first?"

Georgia shook her head. "No."

A slow smile spread over his face as he rose and followed her upstairs.

CHAPTER 24

"I can't believe they sent a private plane," Georgia said, her eyes nearly bugging out when she entered the label's jet. It was luxurious with large, oversized leather seats. She'd been expecting to be crammed into one of the commuter flights that flew daily down to the LA airport.

The flight attendant was dressed in light blue and had champagne flutes on a tray in the front of the plane. She smiled at Georgia and offered her one. Georgia wasn't sure she needed champagne at eight in the morning, but she sure as heck wasn't going to turn it down. This might be her only chance to fly private. She was going to enjoy every moment of it.

"Thank you," she said to the attendant. Once she was seated next to Logan, she leaned over to him and whispered, "They didn't even check my ID."

He chuckled. "It's strange, isn't it?"

"It's the only way to fly," Seth said, sitting across from them. He pressed a button and the chair smoothly reclined.

Levi sat next to him and leaned forward, holding his own

champagne glass. "It's a trip, isn't it? I've flown with Silas a few times, and if there's anything in this world that would make me envy the rich and famous, it's this. Even first class is roughing it compared to this."

Logan chuckled. "It is easy to get used to it fast."

Georgia side-eyed him. "I guess you flew private a lot back when you were touring with your different bands." He sobered, and Georgia wanted to kick herself for bringing up a painful time in his life. "Sorry," she said, squeezing his hand.

"It's all right." Logan leaned over and kissed her temple. "I don't expect you to never mention my past. Yes, we did fly private quite a bit toward the end. It was the only way to get to all the tour dates on time."

Logan was quiet after that, and Georgia decided to let him process his feelings around being involved in the music business again. It wasn't the same as when he was in a band. Publishing was an entirely different thing, but that didn't mean that going back to LA wouldn't take a toll on him.

She turned to Levi. "It's too bad Silas couldn't come."

"Yeah. I would've loved for him to be there when I sign that contract, but he had to get back to the set. His schedule is pretty grueling right now. He was already busy, but then the Oscar nomination came in, and you can imagine that Shannon is working double time trying to field all the offers. It's nice that he has options, but it also means he's having a hard time saying no because there are a lot of high-quality projects." He shrugged. "I'm sure he won't be busy forever."

"He's not the only one who's going to be busy," she said gently.

"Yeah." He sighed. "It's weird because I'm really excited about this new adventure. I thought I knew my path, and then suddenly this drops in my lap. If I didn't love playing with Seth so much, I would've never considered it. Hope and Chad, they're my only real family, and I never imagined leaving Keating Hollow. I love living there. But something tells me if I don't do this, I'll regret it for the rest of my life."

"It's a good reason to go for it," she said. "Following your heart is never the wrong move."

"But am I following my heart?" he asked, a pained expression on his face. "Isn't Silas my heart? He's been asking me to go with him when he's filming on location, but I always say no. I had the internship to keep me busy, but more importantly, I didn't want to go and feel like I was just sitting around waiting for him all the time. And now, here I am, running off to be a musician, something I hadn't ever actually considered. I dropped my internship, will be leaving Hope right when she might need me most, and I'm terrified of what it will do to my relationship with Silas. We already have our rough patches due to his work. I can't imagine this will make it better."

Georgia sympathized with him, but she also knew he was putting a lot of pressure on himself at just eighteen years old. "First thing's first. I assume when you say Hope needs you, you mean because she's considering fostering, right?"

He nodded. "Both of us had really shitty childhoods. I understand why she wants to foster. I was looking forward to trying to make a difference for someone who needed us."

Gods, this kid had a heart of gold. Georgia wanted to scoop him up and hug him for all she was worth. "That's really wonderful of you, Levi. I'm sure you'll still come home to spend time with your sister. If she does get a foster, you'll still be a presence in their life. Even if you're not there physically, you can still be present in their life in a meaningful way.

Technology really has been wonderful for keeping families close over long distances."

"I know," he said with a nod. "And your right. I think I'm just scared about how things might change."

"I get it. Change is hard for all of us. But if you don't step out of your comfort zone, you'll never know what could've been. It's healthy for you to put yourself first. Especially at your age. Hope understands that. And I'm sure Silas does, too."

Levi flushed as he stared down at his full glass of champagne. "He does. Silas couldn't be more supportive."

"That's great."

He nodded. "It is. I just miss him. I really wanted him to be here today."

"I know." She reached out and squeezed his hand. "There will be other special moments though, and if it makes you feel better, you can be my date to the premiere tomorrow night."

"Don't you already have one?" he asked, looking over at Logan.

She shrugged and then winked as she said, "Sure, but who wouldn't want to be escorted by two handsome men?"

He laughed. "I wouldn't say no to that."

Logan suddenly sat up and said, "Georgia, I meant to tell you I got the contract back from my lawyer. We should go over it before we meet the execs in the office."

"Oh, yeah. That sounds like a good idea." She smiled at Levi. "Try not to worry about everything so much. Try to take it all in and just enjoy it for now."

"I will. Thanks, Georgia." He sat back in his seat and finally got to work on sipping his champagne.

∾

LOGAN HAD BEEN ACTING STRANGELY EVER since they'd departed the plane. Georgia watched him as he paced the lobby of the record label. Seth and Levi had already gone into their meeting, and Logan and Georgia were waiting on legal to make the changes his lawyer requested. None of them appeared to be dealbreakers, so they just needed new contracts.

"Excuse me," a woman with blue hair and an eyebrow piercing said. "Sorry to bother you, but are you that singer in the video for "Begin Again"?"

Georgia just stared at her for a moment while she tried to process what she'd said. Video for "Begin Again"? What in the world was she talking about? Maybe Georgia had heard her wrong. "No. I haven't made any music videos. Couldn't have been me."

The woman bit down on her bottom lip as her brow furrowed. "I could swear…" She pulled out her phone and tapped it a few times. "Begin Again" started to play with Georgia singing her heart out. The woman turned her phone so that Georgia could see it. "If this isn't you, then you have a doppelgänger because this woman looks just like you."

Georgia couldn't believe what she was seeing. That was definitely her on the screen. That was video from the day they'd recorded "Begin Again" in the studio with Silas. She fronted the band while she sang her heart out. The emotion rolling off her was intense at moments and really tapped into the bittersweet pain she felt every time she sang it. "How did this get on here?" Georgia asked the woman.

"You mean on YouTube?"

Georgia nodded.

"I'm not sure. Looks like someone leaked it. The account isn't one I recognize. Everyone thinks you and Logan released it yourself. If you did, kudos to you. With how viral this thing is, you'll be in a much better position going into negotiations."

"We've already got the contract worked out," Georgia said. "We're just waiting on legal."

The woman's eyes lit up. "Really? That's amazing. I can't wait to see you live."

"Live? That's not—"

"Gotta go. It was really nice to meet you." She hurried off down the hall and disappeared into one of the offices.

Georgia retrieved her phone, opened YouTube, and searched her name. The video came up immediately. It was trending and was the number three video on the entire site. Georgia sucked in a sharp breath. The fact that it was trending couldn't be an accident. The woman had been correct. Whoever loaded it had done it under a new name, so there was no way to track who they might be. Which meant they had zero audience, and someone was working hard behind the scenes to make sure people saw and clicked on the video.

But why? She glanced up to find Logan staring at her. And then her heart sank. She turned the phone around to show him she'd found the video. "You knew about this, didn't you?"

"Georgia," he started.

She put her hand up. "Yes or no?"

"Yes. I knew." He moved to sit next to her and clasped his hands together as he turned to her.

"Was it you?" Her tone was sharper than she intended, but she couldn't help it. She was pissed as hell. No one had asked her thoughts about if she wanted a video of herself singing online.

"No. I promise it wasn't." He grimaced. "I didn't even realize we were filming that day."

She snorted out her disbelief. "Sure, Logan. I'm supposed to believe that we were recorded accidentally that day when you asked me to sing *and* that our session in the studio was filmed without your knowledge?"

"I know how that sounds. But I really didn't know. Silas saw the switch in the control room for video and hit the button just in case we wanted to see it. I saw the cameras mounted on the walls, but I didn't know they were on that day."

"Okay. Fine. But who did you give it to, and why did they release it online?" She demanded.

"Seth—"

"Ah, Mr. Malone, Ms. Exler, we're ready for you now," a petite blonde in six-inch heels said as she clacked her way over to them. Her hair was styled in an asymmetrical bob, and she had a warm smile on her face. "I can't tell you how happy we are to have you be part of the Desert Sky family."

Logan stood and held his hand out to her. "It's nice to meet you, Ms.—"

She took his hand and said, "Call me Betty."

Georgia stood and shook the woman's hand, wondering who she was at the label. But instead of asking, she was silent as she followed them back to a conference room.

"Have a seat. The team will be in shortly," Betty said and then swept out of the room, leaving Georgia and Logan alone.

"So..." Georgia started. "Seth did something with the video?"

Logan sighed and rubbed his forehead. "This isn't how I wanted this to go down."

She raised her eyebrows. "What does that mean?"

"Seth gave them the recording and also sent along the video recordings," he said.

"Why?" Georgia was genuinely curious. What was the point of sending the footage?

"Because you're gorgeous when you sing, Georgia. You're gorgeous anyway, but when you sing, it's pure magic. You must know that." He was staring at her intently.

"I don't know about magic. But regardless, what does it matter what I look like when I sing? I only recorded the lyrics so another artist can decide if it works for them," she said, trying to ignore the pit forming in her stomach. She didn't know how much Logan was involved in whatever this scheme was, but he'd known about it and hadn't told her. That was bad enough.

He raised his gaze to hers and finally came clean. There was excitement in his eyes, and he couldn't hide the smile trying to claim his lips. "I found out yesterday that the label wants to sign us as another act. You and me. Isn't that amazing? I wanted to surprise you when we got here."

Georgia's stomach rolled, and she seriously wondered if she was going to vomit. "You thought I'd be happy about this?"

The light dimmed in his eyes, and he frowned. "Why wouldn't you be? Didn't you see all the comments on that video? People love you, Georgia. You really touch them with your voice."

"How do I know those comments are real?" she asked defiantly. "Someone did some guerrilla marketing to get it trending like that. They could be commenting using sock puppets."

Logan scoffed. "No way. Just open up Twitter and see how many people are talking about it and linking to it. Maybe there was some serious marketing to get it seen initially, but the interest is real."

Georgia couldn't deny that made her feel good. Who didn't

like being appreciated for something they'd created? But she was pissed as hell that she'd been left out of the loop. Logan had kept information from her, resulting in her getting blindsided at the record label.

The door opened and two men and a woman in business suits strode in. Betty followed, holding a stack of folders.

The woman introduced herself as Penny Kline, and the men were George Pelner and Frank Frankle. Penny asked Betty to pass out the folders and then instructed everyone to take a seat.

"Today has been an exciting day," Penny said, her eyes twinkling. "We couldn't be happier to see so many people responding to your video. That must be exciting, right?"

"Sure," Logan said.

Georgia just shrugged.

"You're not happy with the results?" Penny asked Georgia. "Last I looked it was trending on YouTube and Twitter. For an unknown duo, that's unheard of."

"I'm just surprised by all of this," Georgia said. "I didn't even know until about ten minutes ago that footage of that day even existed. So imagine my surprise to find out someone leaked it online."

Penny pressed a hand to her chest and laughed. "That was just a PR stunt, Georgia. That stuff happens all the time. I'm sure you know that. If anything, the success has helped you and Logan. Your contract terms will be much more favorable with a certified hit on your hands."

Georgia glanced over at Logan. He was watching her intently, and she wondered what he was thinking. She couldn't tell. It was so hard to read him in this situation. And honestly, she didn't think she liked it. "I thought I was coming here to sign a publishing contract, but honestly, I'm not even sure about that now. I don't like to be kept out of the loop."

The three executives stared at her as if she'd just spoken Greek.

Logan cleared his throat. "I'm sorry everyone. This is my fault. Everything happened so fast that Georgia and I didn't get to discuss any of this. Maybe you could give us a rundown on what it is you're offering, and then we can discuss it?"

The three execs all looked at each other with puzzled expressions. There was no doubt they were used to people falling all over themselves to get a contract. Georgia understood it. She'd gone through a time when she was trying to get published with the major book publishers, and it was so difficult to get your foot in the door that most writers would take any contract offered, regardless of how good or bad it might be.

She herself had been offered terrible deals and had considered just biting the bullet in order to try to build her audience. But then self-publishing came along, and she no longer had to worry about getting someone else's approval. All that mattered were the readers. It had been the most freeing decision she'd ever made.

"Okay, sure," Penny said. "Go ahead and open your folders. We do indeed want to offer you a publishing deal. We'd also like to sign the two of you as an act. We'd record an EP first and then send you out on tour with Seth and Levi. The tour would start off as three months but would likely extend to six as long as venues are filling up. Which we're confident they will, since both acts have a fan base already. You would be starting in a very strong position. One that could eventually lead you into superstardom."

"What if I'm not interested in touring?" Georgia asked.

Again, she'd left everyone speechless.

Finally, Penny said, "The tour is what makes you money. If you want to have success in the music industry, you have to tour."

"I see," Georgia said.

"When would we start?" Logan asked.

"You'd start on your EP right away." Frank Frankle said. "I suspect touring will happen in about six months. We'll want to get both acts out while the songs are still relatively new."

"Frank handles the tour side of things," Penny said. "George oversees the material. Everything you write and want to sing goes through him. I'm just the one who signs the checks." She gave them a self-deprecating smile that Georgia suspected was all an act. "So what do you think?"

"Would we have full control over what songs we record?" Logan asked.

"Normally that's not something we'll write into a contract," Penny said.

"What if it was a dealbreaker?" Logan countered.

She chuckled. "I like you. Negotiations are going to be fun. But to answer your question, it's unlikely for the first EP. We'll want marketing in on the decisions so we can make sure we have hit after hit on the record. But if you prove yourself, it's something our top artists have control over."

"Would we have veto power?" Logan asked with one raised eyebrow.

Her lips curved into a sly smile. "We'd never make you record a song you hate."

Logan snorted. "I've heard that before."

She nodded. "It's a concession we can work with."

"Thank you." Logan seemed pleased with himself, but all Georgia could think about was getting out of there. She needed to process the offer and make sure it wasn't something she wanted before she told them all to go to hell. Would she regret it? Maybe. But her situation wasn't the same as Levi's. He was a teenager who was ready to explore the world. Georgia had already done that. Now she was ready for some peace.

"Georgia?" Penny called.

"Yes?" Georgia responded after she shook herself out of her thought process.

"I just wanted to tell you that you have a lovely voice. We'd be honored to have you at our label. You have the contracts. Please have them vetted, and if there are any changes to be made, just let us know and we'll see what we can do." Penny stood, and the other suits stood with her. When Penny got to the door, she glanced back and added, "Just don't make us wait too long. The offer expires in three days."

"Three days?" Logan asked.

"Yes," Penny said. "If we want to capitalize on the leaked video, then we need to move on it right away. We'll need to get started yesterday. So don't sleep on this offer."

They all filed out again, leaving Logan and Georgia alone.

Georgia stood, put the folder in her messenger bag, and walked out without saying another word. Logan was the one who was going to have to do all the talking because she was getting on a plane first thing in the morning and heading back to Keating Hollow.

ogan followed Georgia into the hotel, not sure what to say. He'd really effed up. Why had he thought she'd be so eager to sign a record deal? Because *he* was eager to sign a record deal. Ever since he'd found out Desert Sky wanted them both, he hadn't been able to stop thinking about it.

This wasn't like last time when he'd been dying for the fame. He was past that. No, this was about living without regrets and chasing a dream no matter how late it showed up. He sat down on the edge of the bed and watched as Georgia stood by the window with her arms crossed over her chest.

He needed to say something to help her understand why he wanted this so badly. "Remember when you told Levi on the plane that he had to take chances and follow his dreams no matter where they took him?"

"Yeah," she said wearily.

"That's where I'm at with this offer."

"So you're saying you can't pass it up because you'll always have regrets if you do?" Georgia asked.

"Something like that. Yeah. But there's more. When Cherry died, I pulled back completely. I couldn't even look at my instruments. Or listen to Seth's band that played for hours in our garage. I lost every last desire I had to create music."

"When did it come back?" she asked, looking interested in what he had to say for the first time since they'd left the label.

"After I moved to Keating Hollow, I started to have the desire to play instruments again. It was weird and awkward trying to remember where my fingers were supposed to go, but it turned out I had muscle memory. So I started messing around with just the instruments. It wasn't until I met you that I had that full-on desire to perform again."

"Until you met me?" Georgia asked. She was frowning when she added, "You aren't trying to guilt me into signing anything are you? You don't need me to enjoy music."

"You're right; I don't. And no, I'd never try to guilt you into doing something you don't want to do. But you deserve to know that it's because of our connection when we play that I feel this need to try again."

"Our connection? But what if I say no and don't do this with you?" she countered. "Will you still do it?"

Logan took his time mulling over that question and ultimately nodded. "Yes. While I'd obviously prefer for you to be on stage with me, it's okay if you don't want to. That connection we have? It's reawakened my love for all things music. And if I say no to this, I'll always wonder what could have been."

Georgia moved to sit next to him, appearing to really hear what he had to say. "And what if I told you that the idea of touring, of being on the road all the time, makes my skin crawl?"

He hated hearing that, but he also didn't want to pressure her into anything just because it was what he wanted. "Then I'd have to tell you not to sign their contracts. I don't want you to do anything that makes you unhappy." He took her hand in his and held it with both hands. "I'm sorry about the way things went down today. I was so excited that I never stopped to consider that you'd feel differently. Which is really effing stupid, because I know how much you love Keating Hollow. You've told me before how nervous you get when performing, and I should have realized my dream isn't your dream. I guess I just never thought you'd give up the chance to sing with me every night considering the magic we share."

She gave him a rueful smile. "Are you trying to shame me again?"

He laughed because he knew she was teasing. "Never. I just want to tell my truth."

"And here's mine," she said, her eyes serious for once. "My dream has always been to be a writer. I love it, honestly. Songwriting is sort of in that same space. I like the play on words, trying to figure out what will make for a good verse or bridge. In that sense, I was very much on board with writing songs with you. As for singing, I like it when you're there. Like you said, we have that magic. It's truly wonderful. But I don't care about playing for other people, or cutting records, or even seeing myself go viral on YouTube. I'd be happy playing a song or two with you at the brewery every weekend. But I don't want to live a life on the road. I prefer my space in Keating Hollow. So I guess I'm saying I'm really sorry, but I can't sign a record deal with the label. If I did, I'd be doing it for you, and I'd be miserable."

Logan felt as if his heart was going to break in two. He'd

just found Georgia. He didn't want to give her up. But he also felt as if he couldn't pass up the opportunity to live the life that was stolen from him all those years ago. There was also a nagging voice in the back of his head that told him it was for the best. If he didn't stay with Georgia, she'd be safe. Nothing would happen to her like it did with Cherry and Brit. "If I say no to this, I'll regret it, Georgia. Maybe even start to resent you, because the only reason I'd say no is because it hurts to think about leaving you. And more than anything, I don't want to resent you or live with anymore regrets."

Georgia moved closer and wrapped her arms around him. "Do you think they'll sign you as a solo artist?"

He nodded. "They already told me that based on what they knew about me, they were trying to convince Seth to get me to come back to the industry. I'm sure they'll work something out if it's only me interested."

They sat together for a long time, each of them coming to terms with their decisions. Finally, Georgia said, "I'll still sign the publishing contract if you want. And I'll let them have our song. They can release it with my vocals if they want, but I won't be doing any live performances."

He stared down at her. "Are you sure?"

She nodded. "I love you, Logan. And if there's a chance we can still write songs together, I'm all in. Tell them that a condition of using my vocals is that they give you the same deal they were going to give us. If not, then no deal."

He chuckled. "You're something else. You know that, right?"

She smiled up at him, but there was sadness there. He wanted to take it away, tell her he'd go back to Keating Hollow, forget about his second chance at a music career. But he couldn't. It wasn't fair to either of them.

"You're something else, too, Logan Malone. And I expect front row tickets to all of your shows."

He kissed the top of her head and smoothed her hair back. "Always."

CHAPTER 26

*T*here were tears in Georgia's eyes as she boarded the commercial plane that would take her back to Keating Hollow. She'd decided not to stay for the premiere. It had just been too painful to act like everything was fine when her heart was breaking.

Logan had tried to get her to stay. To enjoy one more night with him before his life was turned upside down, but she'd refused. Instead, she'd held onto him tightly, kissed him, and told him she was rooting for him.

He'd reminded her that they'd be writing songs together, so he'd be back sooner rather than later. They both knew it was a lie. The label had big plans to relaunch him back into the music scene. They were never going to let him disappear for a few weeks to work on new songs with her. They'd have to do everything by Zoom or Facetime. The prospect sounded depressing.

She'd left Logan standing in the doorway of his luxurious hotel room, and now she was sandwiched in the middle seat in coach between a lanky teenager who was taking up all her leg room and a woman who not only talked nonstop but did it while eating. Georgia would be seeing that woman's half-chewed egg salad in her mind for months.

By the time she landed outside of Eureka, exhaustion had kicked in, and it was taking everything she had to hold herself together. What she needed was to be curled up in her own bed, crying her eyes out. But that would have to wait since she needed to figure out a ride back into town.

Georgia had just walked out of the small terminal with her bag in hand when she heard a woman calling her name. "Georgia. Over here!"

She squinted through her tears and spotted Hope Garber waving at her. "Hope?"

"Hi." The other woman smiled gently at her and reached for her bag. "Your friendly Keating Hollow taxi is here to pick you up."

"What?" Georgia genuinely didn't understand. "You're moonlighting as a taxi?"

"No, silly. Levi called and said you could use a ride." She slipped her arm around Georgia and guided her toward the exit. "That is unless you have other plans."

Georgia let out a relieved sigh. "No, not even close. I was going to try a shuttle, but I didn't book in advance because…"

"I know," Hope said. "Don't worry about a thing. I've got you covered."

They climbed into Hope's SUV, and Georgia pressed her head against the cool window.

"You're a lifesaver," Georgia said. "Do you know that?"

"Not literally," Hope teased. "But there's still time."

Normally Georgia would've laughed at her, but she just didn't have it in her. There was nothing left to give.

"Georgia?" Hope asked. "Are you all right?"

She shook her head. "No, but I imagine I will be... eventually."

Hope reached over, squeezed her hand, and then turned the radio up slightly, indicating they didn't need to talk.

Georgia send her a grateful smile before turning to stare out the window at the road leading them back to Keating Hollow.

~

WHEN GEORGIA GOT HOME, she went straight upstairs, intending to climb into her bed. But then she noticed the indentation in the pillow on Logan's side of the bed. She picked it up and hugged it, her tears coming faster when his lingering scent hit her.

"Dammit!" she yelled and threw the pillow across the room. It hit a framed picture, sending it crashing to the floor. It was the one of her and Nick laughing at the beach. A reminder that she'd never gotten her happily-ever-after, and she wasn't getting one now.

She would not be living the life of one of the heroines in her books.

Or could she?

Her aunt's words came back to her. *Write what you want.*

As she sat down at her laptop, Georgia realized that the scene she hadn't been able to get out of her head, with the werewolf going back to his old life, mirrored exactly what happened the day before with Logan. She hadn't even written the passage, and yet, it still happened.

It finally hit her that it didn't matter at all what she wrote or didn't. Life would happen the way it was supposed to. But that didn't mean she couldn't write one hell of a happy ending. One that both she and her heroine deserved.

With her tears dried, Georgia sat down at her desk and let her fingers fly. She didn't let up until the early hours of the next day, but she'd done it. Her hero and heroine had found their way back together again, and the book was finished.

She tapped out an email to her editor, sent it over, and then collapsed into bed, finally feeling at peace about her strange ability to see the future.

CHAPTER 27

*L*ogan was sitting in the corner of the dive bar, sipping a warm beer and wondering what the hell he was doing with his life. It had been three weeks since Georgia had walked out and headed back to Keating Hollow. He'd talked to her a few times, and they'd brainstormed ideas for their next song, but both of them were in pain. And although he always wanted to hear her voice, the breakup was still too fresh, and they both needed some distance just to heal.

"You look terrible," Seth said, flopping into the chair across from him.

Raising his beer in a sarcastic toast, Logan flashed his brother his middle finger.

Seth just laughed. "Still a ray of sunshine, I see."

"You weren't much better when you and Cal broke up," Logan countered.

"Ouch. You wound me." Seth feigned being knifed in the chest.

Logan rolled his eyes. "Don't you need to be somewhere soon? Like that show that starts in ten minutes?"

"Shit. Right. I just came down here to check on you. During the set you seemed really out of it, like disconnected or something. Did you hear from Georgia today?"

"Nope." Someone turned the music up, causing Seth to grimace. "Gotta go, but we're talking more later, got it?"

"Sure," Logan said, knowing the chances of Seth actually instigating the conversation again was slim to none. "Go play. You're gonna rock their socks off, and I can't wait to see it."

Seth grinned at his brother and finally ran backstage, leaving him the eff alone to drink warm beer and feel sorry for himself. Logan knew his brother was right; he *had* been disconnected from the music. It was the second time he'd played live that week and the second time he'd looked out into the crowd and felt absolutely nothing. That contentment that usually washed over him when he was playing was gone. The roar of the crowd meant nothing more than a slight headache. And all he wanted to do was go back to his hotel and call Georgia. But it was late, and she'd be asleep.

Maybe it was the songs he was singing. None of the ones in his set were his own. They were ones written by other songwriters that the label asked him to record. They weren't bad songs. In fact, one was a crowd pleaser that never failed to get them going. It was fun and would probably be played on the radio a lot, but it didn't have the depth of feeling that Logan strived for when he was writing his own music. It just wasn't him.

When Seth and Levi strode out on the stage, the bar erupted in applause. They were who the people had come for. Not Logan. The realization didn't even phase him. He was happy for them. Thrilled even. Their star was taking off just as he knew it would. And when they played their songs, the pair was electric. They had that magic. The magic he was missing since Georgia left.

Logan stood, threw some money on the table for the beer, and left before they even finished their first song.

LOGAN SCANNED the lyrics to the new song the label wanted him to try and groaned. It was a song about a man and his dog from childhood. "This isn't what I meant when I asked if there were any songs with a deeper meaning."

"The songwriter said everything is a metaphor for life," one of the producers explained.

"I'm sure it is, but I'm not singing about a dog like it's my lover. This is just one of the lines I'll never sing: *I miss the warmth of your breath and the weight of your body when you wake me in the morning.*"

One of the sound engineers snickered.

"Okay, okay. That one's out. What about the others?" The producer sounded impatient.

Logan couldn't quite blame him. Not all of the songs were bad. A couple were actually pretty good. But for some reason, Logan just couldn't commit. He sat in one of the leather chairs and ran a hand down his face. "This would go a lot easier if I could sing my own songs."

"Logan, we've been over this. We don't have time for you to write new lyrics before you go out on the road," Penny said from her spot across from him in the sound booth.

If *he went on tour.*

Where had that thought come from? Logan wasn't sure. Did he not want to tour? Judging by how he'd felt during his last couple of gigs, it was a strong possibility. He sighed. "Can't you just give me one afternoon to try to put some lyrics down? I'm just not feeling any of this, and it shows when I'm on stage."

"He's right," Seth said from the doorway.

Logan grinned at him. "When did you get here?"

"Right about the time you refused to sing about a dog molesting you in your bed."

The sound guy snickered again.

"Okay. That's enough," Penny said. "It's the type of song that people will sing along to without even knowing the meaning of the lyrics. Either of you would be lucky to have it. But since you're too high and mighty, I'll send the song off to Randy Giles. He's not above anything, and with his following, it will probably go gold in its first week."

She wasn't wrong. Randy had a massive fanbase that adored him. He could sing about mold in the fridge, and his fans would still show up. Plus, he'd have a lot of fun with it. Penny should've sent it to him first anyway.

"How's it going, brother?" Seth asked.

Logan shrugged. "It could be better. I'm having trouble selecting songs."

"The trouble is that he won't select any," Penny complained. "The only one he seems to like singing is "Begin Again.""

Seth nodded. "That's what I figured." He grabbed Logan by the arm and said, "Let's go. We need to talk."

"But I'm in the middle of something here," Logan protested.

"Not anymore." Penny rose and gathered her things. She glanced at Seth. "Talk some sense into him, will you? We need to get this record moving."

"I'll do my best," Seth assured her. Then he turned his attention back to Logan. "Ready?"

"I don't think I have a choice, do I?"

"Nope." Seth led him out of the sound booth, through the office space, and down the stairs. He didn't stop until they were standing outside on the sidewalk. "Coffee or lunch?"

"Uh, lunch, I guess." Logan couldn't remember if he'd had breakfast or not, but judging by the gnawing in his gut, he figured that was a no. Either way, coffee was out. He didn't need an ulcer on top of everything else.

"This way." He walked across the street into a mom-and-pop deli, ordered two roast beef sandwiches, both on sourdough with spicy mustard, tomatoes and onions. No lettuce. "Fries?"

"Sure." Logan watched him in fascination. This clearly wasn't a brotherly lunch where they sat and caught up with each other. Seth was on a mission and ordering lunch had been caught in the crossfire.

"Two ice teas, no sweetener, and one coffee," Seth added.

"Are you doubling down on the caffeine?" Logan asked him when he set one of the ice teas and the coffee in front of himself.

"Yes. I'd hook up an IV if that were a thing. I didn't get in until four this morning."

"Sounds like you and Levi had an awesome show," Logan said.

Seth grinned. "It was off the hook. Too bad you missed it. You didn't even stay to hear us play "Begin Again.""

Logan's eyes widened. "You played Georgia's song? How did it go over? Did the crowd like it?"

Seth's lips twitched. "They loved it, brother. It was their favorite of the night. You should hear Levi belt out some of those notes. It's really something."

"Now I regret leaving," Logan said, almost meaning it. Surely if the song was that good, someone would've recorded it and put it on YouTube by now. He'd search for it later. "Though I was in bed by ten-thirty, so not all was lost."

"You're a really sad sack, you know that?" Seth said, shaking his head. "In bed by ten-thirty. What are you, eighty?"

Logan chuckled. "You just wait. A few more years and you'll be hugging your pillow before the late-night shows air, too."

"I doubt it, but whatever you say."

Their food arrived, and the conversation stopped while they dug into their sandwiches. But when Seth was finished with the first half of his, he put the rest down and leaned in. "What's going on with you?"

"What do you mean?" Logan asked just to stall the conversation because he didn't know what to say.

"You know exactly what I mean. You're not happy with the songs. You're not happy recording. And you certainly aren't happy performing, which I have to say is really freakin' weird, because I remember what you used to be like onstage. You were so into it. It was as if the music just spoke to people through you. But now? You're just up there going through the motions. You sound good. No one could deny that, but your drive to put on a show seems to be MIA."

That's because it was. And he didn't know how to get it back. Logan sighed. "I don't know, man. I really don't."

"Then let me ask you this… Do you really want to be here doing this?"

"Yes," he said automatically. It was his dream, wasn't it?

Seth raised a skeptical eyebrow. "Are you lying to me or to yourself?"

Logan leaned back in his chair and crossed his arms over his chest. "Why are you doing this?"

"Why are you?" Seth countered.

"Because you forced me to have lunch with you," Logan all

but growled. "You pulled me out of my session, for what? To try to get me to quit?"

Seth's jaw tightened as anger flashed in his blue eyes. "Do you really think I'd try to get you to quit my tour? That I don't want you there? Are you serious right now? I want nothing more than to tour the country with my brother. It sounds effing awesome. But I don't want to do that if it's making you miserable. Because make no mistake, brother, that's what you are. Is it Georgia? Is it because she's not here?"

Probably. Maybe.

Logan found himself shaking his head. "I do want her here. And I miss her like crazy, but I don't think that's it. At least not directly. I'm sure if she was here, everything would be different. When we sing together, everything just falls into place. I feel like I'm *home* with her, you know?"

"Sure. I've seen it in action," he agreed.

"When she decided she didn't want this life, I had to accept that, and I have. I get it. But because she passed, I had to decide whether to go back to Keating Hollow and wonder what would've been or go for it. I've been passionate about music my entire life. I don't need that magic we created to love it. So here I am, giving it my best shot."

Seth snorted. "No you aren't. Not even close."

Logan scowled. "What does that mean?"

"It means you're not giving it your best shot. You're just going through the motions." He gave Logan a sympathetic smile. "The question is, why? I know how much you used to love recording songs and performing. More often than not, they weren't your original lyrics when you were with the label. What happened this time around? Most of the songs are good, despite the dog porn one."

Logan couldn't help but laugh. Then he sobered. "I don't know. I really don't. I'm just not feeling any of them."

"Could it be that your dream changed?" Seth asked gently. "Maybe it isn't to be a rock star anymore."

"That's not for you to say," Logan said, irritation getting the better of him.

"No, it isn't. But I think it's something you should ask yourself before you sign those final contracts later this week."

"You think I made the wrong choice, leaving Georgia to pursue an old dream?" Logan asked him.

"No, I don't. You had an opportunity, and if you'd turned it down, you would've always wondered. But now that you're in the thick of it, maybe you've had your questions answered. I don't know, Logan. I just see you struggling while I'm on top of the world. I want that for you. I want you to love your life with no regrets. If you do this, will you regret walking away from Georgia and your writing career?"

"I didn't walk away from either," Logan insisted.

Seth stared him down. "Didn't you, though?"

"No." He would never walk away from Georgia. At least not for good. He couldn't.

"If you say so." Seth picked up the other half of his sandwich and took a bite. Apparently the talking portion of the lunch was over.

CHAPTER 28

*G*eorgia lay on the couch, staring up at the ceiling. Was that a spider web? She really should think about hiring someone to clean. Because the thought of brooming the ceiling downright depressed her.

It had been three weeks since she finished her latest book, and besides dealing with edits and revisions, she hadn't done any other work. She did have intimate knowledge of the inside of her refrigerator and pantry though. It was amazing how many packages of cookies she'd had stored in the back. Unfortunately, the cookies were all gone and her fridge was mostly empty. The only snacks left were a jar of peanut butter and some stale tortilla chips.

She'd go shopping later. There was always takeout. And leftovers from Thanksgiving if she managed to make it to the Townsends' family home. It was just a few days away, and they'd invited her, but that meant she'd have to put on clean clothes and brush her hair.

A knock sounded on her door, and she rolled over with a

groan. Maybe if she pretended she wasn't home they'd go away.

No such luck. When she didn't answer the knock, whoever it was tried the doorbell. Over and over again.

"Okay, fine! I'm coming." She slipped off the couch, caught a whiff of some unpleasant body odor, and wrinkled her nose. Maybe her stench would serve as a repellent for whoever was interrupting her brooding. She yanked the door open to find Hope standing on her porch with her hands on her hips. "Hope, uh, hi. What are you doing here?"

"I came to save you from yourself." She strode in without an invitation and headed for the couch, where old cookie wrappers and empty popcorn bags were warring for space with her empty sparkling water cans. "Is this what you've been eating all week?"

"Pretty much. I decided to just eat what's here and work down the pantry before shopping again."

"Or showering?" she asked with her eyebrows raised.

"You were supposed to ignore that fact," Georgia said, not even upset. It was true. She didn't remember the last time she'd stepped into the shower. Two, maybe three… oh, no… four days? It hadn't been an entire week, she knew that much, because she always shaved her legs on Fridays.

"Friends don't let friends wallow in their own filth. Now go take a shower and get dressed. You're getting out of here today even if it kills both of us." She grabbed one of the empty popcorn bags and used it as a trash bin for the rest of the empty food containers cluttering the coffee table.

Georgia's manners kicked in, and she tried to take the bag from her guest. "I'll get that. You have a seat while I—"

Hope snatched it back. "Nope. I've got this. Your only job is to shower and get dressed. Go."

"You seem a little aggressive today," Georgia mused.

"Do I?" she asked innocently. "Wait until you see what I do if you don't head upstairs to the shower."

Her sass made Georgia laugh for the first time in days. Maybe weeks. "Fine. I'm going. But don't touch the kitchen. I'll handle it when I get back down."

"Mm-hmm." Hope waved toward the stairs and then carried her load of garbage into the kitchen.

Once Georgia was under the spray of the hot water, she wondered why she'd waited so long. She stayed under the spray for longer than necessary, rationalizing that she'd already conserved water by not showering the previous four, maybe five, days. By the time she was done, dressed, and had her hair presentable to the world again, she'd been upstairs for a good forty-five minutes.

"Hope?" she called from the bottom of the stairs. "Sorry I took so—what happened in here?" All of the garbage was gone, the blankets had been folded and placed on the couches artfully for a pop of color, her coffee table had been cleaned, and her carpet had fresh vacuum lines. "Did I hire a maid and forget?"

Hope came out of the kitchen, eyed Georgia, and said, "Perfect timing. Let's go."

Georgia inched toward the kitchen and noticed the mountain of dishes had been done and her counters gleamed. "I told you not to touch the kitchen."

Hope rolled her eyes. "What are you going to do? Send me a bill for disrupting your mess?"

"Ha-ha. Thank you. You really didn't need to do that. I would've gotten around to it eventually," Georgia insisted as she followed Hope outside.

"I know. I wanted to," she said and nodded toward the

sparkling purple golf cart parked behind Georgia's Audi. "Hop in. We're going for a ride."

"To where?" Georgia did as she was told, mostly because it was just easier than arguing. But she did have to admit that the late-November sun on her face was really nice. She should really get outside more. Maybe start a winter garden. Or something a little less ambitious like taking a daily walk around the neighborhood. Surely she wouldn't fall and fracture her foot while using the sidewalk, right? Because there wasn't anyone in Keating Hollow to carry her around anymore. She needed to be more careful.

"The river." Hope glanced over at her. "Buckle up."

"Yes, ma'am." Georgia secured her seatbelt and then proceeded to be completely obnoxious as she demanded that Hope floor it and do donuts around the Toyota stopped at a traffic light in front of them. "You're no fun," she declared when Hope ignored her.

Hope snorted. "I'm fun. I'm lots of fun. But not when I'm driving. Safety first."

"This is the worst golf cart race ever," Georgia pouted.

"Are you drunk or something? It's not a race unless there's another golf cart to race against, Georgia."

"No, just slightly crazy from not seeing anyone for three weeks. I did name the spider on my ceiling though. Webster. He and I have gotten close, though he doesn't appreciate the fact that I keep telling him his web has to go."

"Webster?" Hope said and rolled her eyes. "So original."

"Thanks, I try," Georgia said, refusing to take the bait to argue the spider's name.

Goddess above, maybe she *was* drunk. Did she finish off the champagne that morning? Or was it yesterday? She had no idea. All the days had started to blend together.

Finally, after what seemed like hours, though it was likely only minutes, Hope drove the golf cart down to the river where another orange golf cart was waiting.

"Ohhhh," Georgia exclaimed. "We really are having golf cart races!"

"Nope. Not today. But I do have another surprise for you." She pulled the cart up close to the other one and gestured to the driver.

"Logan!" Georgia cried and nearly fell out of the cart as she tried to scramble to him. "What are you doing here?"

He took her hand and helped her into the cart to sit next to him. Once she was seated, he didn't let go of her hand. Instead, he did that thing where he held it with both of his hands, making her feel like he was never going to let go. "I was sitting in the park yesterday thinking about all the things we did together here in Keating Hollow and all the things you suggested but we didn't have time for. The one thing you mentioned that I really wanted to do was participate in the famous golf cart races."

Georgia glanced over her shoulder at the cart Hope was driving. She'd just turned onto Main Street and looked like she might be headed to A Touch of Magic. "I think our second cart has gone MIA."

He chuckled. "Everyone is working right now, but Hope had about an hour to help me out. While there won't be any racing today, we will take a ride and hopefully work out a few things."

"Work out what things? Like when I'll get to see you again?" she asked hopefully. Because she was certain this was going to be a quick trip. His schedule was too tight for him to be running back and forth from LA to Keating Hollow all the time.

"More like how often we're going to have date night, which mornings we'll take hikes in the redwoods, and how often you allow me to sleep over before you start making me pay rent."

Georgia felt a tingle of hope blossom from somewhere deep inside of her. "What exactly are you saying?"

His lips quirked with amusement. "Just that I plan on being around a lot more and want to know how often I can see you before you start throwing me out of your space."

The bubble of hope grew from a pea to a watermelon. But she sure wasn't going to count her chickens yet. "What about your record deal? Aren't you supposed to be on the road in a few months?"

He shook his head. "No tour. No record."

Georgia stiffened and then turned to face him with a sick feeling of devastation weighing down her limbs. "Did those bastards drop you after all your hard work? They can't do that. There were contracts. They made both of us promises. They aren't going to get away with this. We'll sue, or at least threaten to sue and make it all public. What about Levi and Seth? Are they still touring or—"

"Georgia," he said, softly cutting her off. "Everything is fine. Levi and Seth are still good to go. In fact, they are adding dates for them left and right. As for me, the contracts aren't actually signed. I asked them for changes and they agreed, but legal was dragging their feet. Which was fine. I was still working out what songs I wanted to do. But then Seth said some things to me that made me really think. And in the end, I realized that touring the country and living the life of a rock star was my old dream, not my current one."

Her heart felt as if it was going to beat right out of her chest. Did she just hear him correctly? "You're saying *you* backed out?"

He nodded and lifted her hand to kiss her knuckles. "I was miserable and too stubborn to realize why."

"Don't say you backed out because of me. I don't want to be the reason you miss out on something so huge." A soft breeze picked up, and she shivered slightly.

Logan reached into the back seat of the golf cart, grabbed a sweatshirt, and handed it to her. "Here. This should help."

Georgia gratefully pulled it on and was rewarded with the faint scent of his cologne. "It smells like you," she said, smiling shyly. "I like that."

"I like that you like that." He cleared his throat. "But back to our discussion. I didn't back out because of you. I did it because of me. I hated almost everything about it. From having to sing songs the label wanted me to sing, to performing two to three nights a week and living out of a hotel. In my younger days, I would've endured all that and more for success. But now? I want to sing and write songs I love, not ones that will sell well. I also don't want to be spending all my nights in a loud bar when all I really want is to be with you. It just isn't what I thought it would be, and as it turns out, I don't need it. Or even want it."

"Wow. You gave it a shot at least. No regrets?" she asked.

"None at all."

"But you might regret it later," she said, trying to cover all the bases.

"I doubt it," he said and wrapped his arm around her shoulder. "Not when everything I truly want is right here in my arms."

Georgia felt hot tears prick her eyes. "You mean it? Really? You're staying here in Keating Hollow with me?"

"I mean it," he said and dipped his head so that their lips

were just inches apart. "What do you say, Georgia? Friday night date-nights and Sunday brunch every week?"

"I don't know. Every week seems like quite the commitment. I'll have to check my calendar," she teased.

"Can I at least get your Friday nights and Sunday mornings for the rest of the year?" he asked.

"Yes," she whispered. "Definitely, yes."

Logan kissed her again, taking his time to make sure she knew just how much he'd missed her.

When they broke apart, she whispered, "Welcome home."

CHAPTER 29

$\mathcal{L}$ ogan rose early in the morning of the winter solstice and silently made his way into his kitchen, careful to not wake Georgia. She was curled up in his bed, sleeping soundly after they spent half the night working on another song.

They still had their publishing contract at Desert Sky and wrote songs when one of them had an idea. This one had come from Georgia and had started with just one word, *dreamer*. By the time they were done, they were both convinced it could hit the top of the pop charts. Levi and Seth had added their vocals to Georgia's on the track "Begin Again" and had added the song to their album. There was a good chance it was going to go multi-platinum and win important music awards.

Georgia didn't care so much about the awards or even the prestigious magazine articles. All she wanted to do was write her books and some songs and spend time with Logan. After being back in town for just a few days, he wondered why he'd ever left in the first place. He supposed that he was so caught up in what he'd lost all those years ago when Cherry died, that once his music found him again, he'd had to get it back.

It had been jarring to realize that he'd spent years mourning the loss of a career that he didn't even particularly like. It had taken Seth's words and desire for him to be happy for Logan to see it. But once he had, he hadn't wasted any time. He'd let the label know he was out, packed that same day, and enlisted help from Hope so that he could surprise the love of his life.

Logan smiled to himself as he worked on making blueberry pancakes for Georgia. He'd learned a few days ago that she had a weakness for them. And today he needed all the help he could get.

When the pancakes were done and he had them plated on a tray along with freshly squeezed orange juice and coffee, he placed the little box right where the fork should go so that she didn't miss it and then made his way back into his bedroom.

He smiled when he spotted her peeking up at him through sleepy eyes. "I didn't wake you, did I?"

"No," she said with a yawn. "Not at all." Her eyes darted to the tray he'd left on the dresser. "Is that what I think it is?"

"Depends. What do you think it is?" he asked, wondering if she'd already figured out the surprise.

"Uh, blueberry pancakes. Hand them over, buddy. And fair warning, I'll probably hoover them off the plate, so if that turns you off, don't watch."

Logan let out a hardy laugh. "If it did, you'd have scared me away a long time ago."

"Yeah, I can see that." She grinned and reached for the tray. "Lucky for me— What's that?" She looked up from the tray and back down at the little box then back up at him again. "Logan? What's in the box?"

"You'll need to open it to find out," he said.

She stared at it and shook her head. "No. I can't."

"Why not?" he asked, both amused and more than a little nervous.

"Because if it isn't what I think it is, I'm not sure I'll handle it well."

He took the tray from her hands and placed it on the bed. Then he picked up the box, shook it a little, and said, "Georgia Exler, will you move in with me?"

"Move in?" she squeaked out. "Here?"

"Yes, here. With me in case that wasn't clear," he confirmed.

"Oh." She blew out what had to have been a disappointed breath and nodded. "Yes. I'm here almost all the time anyway. It makes sense I move my clothes in."

Her disappointment was killing him. He'd meant this to be fun, not an unconscious judgment of their relationship. "There's a key for you," he prompted.

"Okay. I'll put it on my chain later." She kissed him on the cheek. "That was very thoughtful of you, and thank you for the kick-ass pancakes. Love them."

"Georgia," he said, waiting for her to look at him.

"Yeah?" She said as she stuffed a bite of pancake in her mouth.

"How do you feel about marriage?" he asked, ready to move this moment along at any cost.

"In general or for myself?" she asked him.

"For yourself."

"I guess I've always seen myself in the big white dress and in a home on the hillside with a view of the mountains. My husband has to be responsible but also ready to spoil me a little. He also has to be witty. Those are my dealbreakers."

Logan nodded. "Sounds like I have a head start since I have a house on the hillside with a view of the mountains."

"I put that in there so you'd be in the lead," Georgia admitted.

"Good. I need it today." Logan got down on one knee, grabbed the ring box off the tray, opened it and held the antique ring that had been his grandmother's out to her. "Georgia Exler, will you marry me?"

Her lips curved into that smile he loved so much as she simply said, "Yes."

CHAPTER 30

*B*rinn Taylor walked into her cousin Wanda's house feeling like a million bucks. It had been a long time since she'd dressed up for anything, much less a themed winter solstice party. She didn't really like large parties, instead preferring small, intimate gatherings. But the party was both a solstice bash as well as the official housewarming for Wanda and Cameron's new place.

The invitation had specified that guests should dress up like a famous couple from the movies. If they didn't have a date, a name would be provided. Brinn had gotten Rose from *Titanic*. Wanda had gone all out, making sure Brinn had the right hair, the right dress and shoes, and last but not least, the jewelry. She of course had opted for the fake Hope Diamond.

Everything was perfect, much like Wanda's brand-new home. It was just outside of town on Cameron's family farm near the Pelsh Winery. They had views of the grape vines, the river, and the mountains. Brinn had joked a couple of times about moving into her guest room. Knowing Wanda, if Brinn had been serious, Brinn would already be living there. She was just that type of person.

"Brinn! Look at you!" Wanda called as she hurried over to her. "You're gorgeous. I can't believe you found that lace dress at a consignment shop. It looks exactly like the one from the movie."

"You don't look too bad yourself." Wanda was dressed up in a sparkling black velvet dress and had her hair styled like Tess from *Working Girl*. "Your shoulders are incredible."

Wanda beamed. "I made the party a theme just because I wanted to wear this dress. Genius, right?"

Brinn laughed at her. "You always find a way to get what you want."

"Speaking of getting what I want," she said, eyeing Cameron, her screenwriter husband, as he made his way to them. Sure enough, he was dressed as Jack Trainer from the same movie, only his look wasn't nearly as iconic. Still, he had his shirtsleeves rolled up and was rocking pretty good forearms.

Brinn waved to Cameron and told her cousin, "I'll be back. I think I need something from the bar."

"Have at it, and don't forget to mingle!" Wanda called after her.

"I mingle," Brinn muttered under her breath. Her cousin was extremely extroverted, and when anyone who was more on the quiet side was around, Wanda saw it as her duty to draw them out. That was nice sometimes, but she didn't need to be babysitting Brinn at the party. Brinn could manage on her own.

The residents of Keating Hollow did not disappoint. Almost everyone in town was at the party, and they were dressed up as everyone from Sonny and Cher to Romeo and Juliet. Her favorite couple, though, was Levi and Silas. They'd come as Harry Potter and Draco Malfoy. Two thumbs up for fan fiction.

Brinn made the rounds, chatting with Yvette and Jacob, Abby and Clay, Noel and Drew, and Shannon and Brian before she peopled herself out and had to find a corner to recharge. She watched from her cozy area as Georgia and Logan announced their engagement. They both glowed with happiness, and Brinn wondered if she'd ever find love like that again or if it was one of those things that only came around once and that was it.

Considering it had been close to five years since her only serious relationship had ended, she was leaning on the side of yes. You only get one.

Brinn sighed, knowing she was self-sabotaging. What did she need a man for anyway? She was Rose from *Titanic.* She'd take a page out of her book and start doing all the things on her bucket list, even if it meant going by herself because everyone she knew was either having babies or working crazy hours. There weren't many people who had time to go to a welding class in the middle of the day.

"Brinn, hi!" Georgia said as she rushed over. The gorgeous author and her fiancé were dressed up like Jeannie and Major Nelson. Georgia was adorable in her billowy pants and short velvet vest over a silky bustier. Of course Logan was dashing in his Air Force uniform. "Love this," Georgia said, gesturing to Brinn's beaded dress.

"Thanks. You look great, too." She grinned at her. Brinn had always liked Georgia. They'd first met when Georgia came for Miranda Moon's first book signing at Hollow Books. She'd been sweet, engaging, and just really kind. That wasn't always the case. "I hear congratulations are in order. Let me see the ring."

Georgia held her antique ring out with pride. "I love it. It belonged to Logan's grandmother."

The ring really was very beautiful, and Brinn spent time chit-chatting with them about their new songs, new books, and other projects they were involved in. Then they were called away, and Brinn saw her escape. She'd come. She'd spoken with her cousin and plenty of the Townsend clan. Now all she wanted was a hot bath and a holiday movie on Netflix.

Brinn had just about reached the door when she heard, "If you jump, I jump."

She spun around and found a Jack lookalike. He was wearing brown pants, suspenders, a button-down shirt, and black dress shoes. To top it off, he had the blond hair that fell over one eye. "Hello there, Jack Dawson," she said, playing along. "You're looking handsome this—" She abruptly stopped talking when she looked into Jack Dawson's eyes and realized the man behind the costume was none other than Austin Steele.

Austin Steele, the love of her life.

The same Austin Steele who'd skipped town five years earlier without even leaving a note.

The one who had ripped her heart out and crushed it.

It'd been weeks since she'd run into him at the healer's office, and she'd successfully avoided him ever since. She didn't know why he'd returned to Keating Hollow, but she didn't intend to find out.

"Excuse me," Brinn said. "I have somewhere to be."

"Aww, don't go yet, Rose." There was a mischievous glint in his eye when he added, "You haven't even asked me to draw you like one of my French girls."

Brinn's cheeks flushed hot with embarrassment as she thought of that night long ago when she'd asked him to do just that. If she'd been anywhere else other than her cousin's party, she would have told him where he could shove the sketchbook he was holding. Instead, she held her head up high, walked right past him, and said, "Don't hold your breath, Mr. Dawson. I don't give second chances."

DEANNA'S BOOK LIST

Witches of Keating Hollow:

Soul of the Witch
Heart of the Witch
Spirit of the Witch
Dreams of the Witch
Courage of the Witch
Love of the Witch
Power of the Witch
Essence of the Witch
Muse of the Witch
Vision of the Witch
Waking of the Witch
Honor of the Witch

Witches of Christmas Grove:

A Witch For Mr. Holiday
A Witch For Mr. Christmas
A Witch For Mr. Winter

Premonition Pointe Novels:

Witching For Grace

Witching For Hope

Witching For Joy

Witching For Clarity

Witching For Moxie

Witching For Kismet

Miss Matched Midlife Dating Agency:

Star-crossed Witch

Honor-bound Witch

Outmatched Witch

Jade Calhoun Novels:

Haunted on Bourbon Street

Witches of Bourbon Street

Demons of Bourbon Street

Angels of Bourbon Street

Shadows of Bourbon Street

Incubus of Bourbon Street

Bewitched on Bourbon Street

Hexed on Bourbon Street

Dragons of Bourbon Street

Pyper Rayne Novels:

Spirits, Stilettos, and a Silver Bustier

Spirits, Rock Stars, and a Midnight Chocolate Bar

Spirits, Beignets, and a Bayou Biker Gang

Spirits, Diamonds, and a Drive-thru Daiquiri Stand

Spirits, Spells, and Wedding Bells

Ida May Chronicles:

Witched To Death
Witch, Please
Stop Your Witchin'

Crescent City Fae Novels:
Influential Magic
Irresistible Magic
Intoxicating Magic

Last Witch Standing:
Bewitched by Moonlight
Soulless at Sunset
Bloodlust By Midnight
Bitten At Daybreak

Witch Island Brides:
The Wolf's New Year Bride
The Vampire's Last Dance
The Warlock's Enchanted Kiss
The Shifter's First Bite

Destiny Novels:
Defining Destiny
Accepting Fate

Wolves of the Rising Sun:
Jace
Aiden
Luc
Craved
Silas
Darien

Wren

Black Bear Outlaws:
Cyrus

Chase

Cole

Bayou Springs Alien Mail Order Brides:
Zeke

Gunn

Echo

ABOUT THE AUTHOR

New York Times and USA Today bestselling author, Deanna Chase, is a native Californian, transplanted to the slower paced lifestyle of southeastern Louisiana. When she isn't writing, she is often goofing off with her husband in New Orleans or playing with her two shih tzu dogs. For more information and updates on newest releases visit her website at deannachase.com.

Made in the USA
Las Vegas, NV
08 February 2022

43413558R00142